Mary's Field

Millennial Mind Publishing
2389 South, 300 East, Salt Lake City, Utah 84115
www.american-book.com
Printed in the United States of America on acid-free paper.

Mary's Field

Designed by Stuart Smith, stusmith@ntlworld.com

Publisher's Note: *This is a work of fiction. Names, characters, places, and incidents either are the product of the author's imagination or, are used fictitiously, and any resemblance to actual persons, living or dead, events, or locales is entirely coincidental.*

Library of Congress Cataloging-in-Publication Data is available upon request.

ISBN 1-930586-76-0

Peters, Vic, Mary's Field

Special Sales

These books are available at special discounts for bulk purchases. Special editions, including personalized covers, excerpts of existing books, and corporate imprints, can be created in large quantities for special needs. For more information e-mail orders@american-book.com or call 1-800-296-1248.

Mary's Field

By Vic Peters

Dedication

For Nonie

Forward

When the Holy Spirit comes, listen.

Chapter One

Over time, the garden of a man's life will reveal pieces of things that were planted, traces of what has visited, and the eternal power of what gives life to all. This is true of all gardens, no matter their success or failure.

"Under there, Mary! See it? Get the darn thing!"
Mary rolled over and turned on the light beside their bed. Whatever had scurried through the darkness was now gone.

"Everything okay?" his wife asked.

"Yeah," he answered while scratching his short black hair and moving his eyes around the room, trying to sort out realities.

"Was it the cat again?" Mary asked.

For the past few nights, Jim had been awakened by what he thought was a cat running across their bed. Last night he felt it curl up and sleep beside his leg.

"Yeah, but it didn't come alone."

"What do you mean not alone? There were two of them?"

He waited for a second, reliving the experience. The dream seemed so real to him that he was having trouble believing that it didn't happen.

"No, not two cats, just the one. But it felt like…like someone just sat down on the end of the bed, you know? I could feel somebody sitting there." Jim turned toward her, not squinting from the light anymore. "What bothers me, Mare, is that I get the feeling that I should know the person. I mean, I'm not afraid or anything. Follow me?"

Mary half nodded at him, caught in a yawn. "Well, your mom says that it is…"

"What?" he interrupted with a frown. "You told my mom about my dreams? Oh, for Pete's sake, now that old woman will be callin' the psychic hotline or somethin'!" Mary reached over and pushed her husband a little.

"You big baby. I'll tell whomever I want. You're the crazy one, not me."

He couldn't help but sort of laugh at her a little; it always made him laugh when she called him a big baby.

"Fine. Then go on ahead and call my little sister while you're at it. She'd love this." He stood up and stretched. "I'm gonna get a shower. I won't be able to sleep anymore."

She was reaching for the phone when he grabbed her.

Revealing itself in the early moonlight, a thin white blanket of frost had settled upon the pumpkins in their garden. Tomatoes hung their heads low, waiting for the sun to release them from winter's early grip. And a maple leaf, whose color echoed a springtime daffodil of long ago, was finally freed to dance with the breeze that it had only caressed.

"Fancy meeting you here," she said, blocking his way to the kitchen table.

Jim grinned, knowing what she was up to.

"Where's my kiss?"

"Hmmm…do I know you?"

She waited, unimpressed.

"Come here." He winked. "I was just kiddin'."

Mary accepted his embrace. He pulled her closer, taken in by her smell. His hand slid down her short green silk nightgown, swirled along its hem and tried to sneak up the inside of it.

SLAP! The spatula that she had been holding smacked against his backside.

"I think you've had quite enough of that. Now sit your butt down at that table or else."

Jim stumbled backwards, rubbing his rear, feigning injury with practiced playfulness.

The darkness outside allowed him to observe the reflection of him and his kitchen in the window as he sat down at the table, waiting for her to bring him what she had cooked. He didn't see the lines of age growing around his tan face, or the wide strong jaw of his father or even the flecks of gray starting along the sides of his head; rather, he watched his wife. Mary was everything to Jim—his ideal woman—and even after twenty years of marriage, he never grew tired of looking at her. Perhaps the quality he liked best in his wife was her ability to transform their home into a comfortable and inviting place. She was a nest maker.

After serving him a plate, she joined her husband with a cup of coffee in a big blue mug.

"So, you want to talk about it?"

"The dream? Oh, I dunno. What's to talk about? It's just weird is all, and…"

Mary was listening, but looking at him as well, all of him. Even at forty, Jim was in almost perfect condition, the result of years of hard physical work.

"And?"

"And I feel like somethin' is gonna happen, Mare, and…"

"And what?"

"And nuthin'."

"Oh," she sassed back, rolling her eyes.

Jim watched his wife, knowing that she was attempting to pry his thoughts out of him, and he evaded her.

"You gonna flip that thing or you want me to call the fire department and have them do it for you?" He motioned with his head toward the stove where another pancake was burning.

"Rats!" Mary jumped up from the table.

Jim sat shaking his head, watching his little woman pry the charcoal remains off of the grill onto the plate with the other "mistakes."

The irony was that his dad was a fantastic cook, but Jim ended up falling in love with a girl who just couldn't keep things on the light side of black. Maybe she wasn't big enough, he mused, rubbing a hand on his clean-shaven face. The stove did seem to outsize her petite frame.

A black lab outside pressed her nose against the glass door and wagged her tail. She knew that smell: breakfast time. Jim used to like to joke to his friends that his dog was once a yellow lab, but changed colors from eating all of his wife's mistakes.

It wasn't much longer before he was filling up his thermos and heading out the door. As he passed by Mary, his free hand slipped up her nightgown again, which gained him not the quick move to second base he was going for, but only a loud shriek.

"Whaddya think yer doin?" she asked, holding up the spatula for self defense.

Jim eyed the spatula. "On second thought, I'll see you tonight, my dear!" he said with a rather poor evil laugh and turned to walk out the door.

"Hey, mister! Where's my kiss?" she asked, giving him "the look." All married guys know "the look," especially Jim. The two of them had been going out together since the eleventh grade.

He noticed it right off. "That ain't 'the look,' girl. I know 'the look.' That's a pretend look. You want me," he laughed, "don't cha?"

Jim made a goofy face and tried to kiss her, but she swung her head to the side, whacking him in the face with her blond ponytail.

Rule number one: Don't blow off "the look," not even a pretend one.

"Hah!" she said with a playful laugh. "Take that, you pervert!"

Jim was considering putting down his things and chasing her around the house for a while, just to remind her what kind of pervert he could be, but he knew he didn't have the time.

She looked up at him with exasperation. "One kiss," she said, holding up a finger. "A nice kiss, got it?" Mary put her hands on her hips, tilting her head back.

Jim took notice of the spatula still in her hand. "Fine," he conceded, and gave her a quick chicken peck on the cheek.

"Funny. What are you? My aunt?" she snapped.

He made his voice sound like an old witch's and pointed at her. "I'll get you my pretty," he said, his hand dropping to point at her hemline, "and your little fuzzy, too!"

Half running, trying to get away from the psycho, spatula-swinging woman he adored, Jim made it to the safety of the morning's darkness where his impatient dog was waiting. He paused just long enough to let the dog get a sniff and gave her a scratch behind the ears.

"See ya later, you old fat charcoal eatin' dawg. Git inside now. That old woman has got some more colorin' for ya."

"I heard that," Mary yelled from the kitchen window and shook the spatula at him. "And I'll collect on that kiss, with interest!"

The dog wagged her tail, trotting on in as Jim went out.

Minutes later, standing on her tiptoes, Mary watched out of her window, seeing the truck headlights turn the corner as he left, and somehow knowing that he had spilled his coffee again. She sort of smiled at the thought and found herself saying the same thing she did most every work morning.

"Please look out for him and bring him back home safe to us." While she spoke, she held onto a tiny gold cross necklace.

Almost on cue, Jim was busy cursing the coffee cup that was rolling around on the passenger side floorboard, empty now, of course. Today it was Jim's Speech Number Eighteen, the one about how he was going to get a cup holder, but he never would as it was just another of his special quirks. The old blue '68 Chevy pickup swerved from one lane to the other while he tried in vain to pick the cup up, missing the same row of apple trees he just missed several times a week.

He gave up, promising to himself to remember that the cup was lodged between the seat and the other door.

"Click" went the bluegrass tape as he popped it into the machine. Jim turned it up and his fingers started following the banjo rolls. Soon enough he was singing along in a twangy hillbilly voice.

"Out off in a wooded cabin, is where my Corey dwells, ya know she makes that bootleg liquor and what she doesn't drink she sells..., Say dig a hole, Dig a hole in the meddaw, Dig a hole in the cold cold ground...Dig a hole, Dig a hole in the meddaw, gonna lay Darlin' Corey down."

The song broke into an instrumental and Jim continued playing his invisible banjo while stomping the floorboards with his left foot.

"Wake up, wake up, Darlin' Corey, what makes you sleep so sound? Ya know them revenuers' a comin', gonna tear your still-house down..."

Jim kept up his stomp and holler routine until he wheeled into the gravel parking lot of the shed for the county highway department.

The door shut with a slam and Jim walked along the front of an old log building toward a smaller makeshift shack around back. There were men already mustered around a burn barrel while their daily job assignments were being handed out.

"Jimbo!" boomed a tall slender brown-haired man named Harrison, trying to be heard over the rumble of diesel engines. "We missed you this morning. What happened?"

Jim was a little embarrassed. He usually met with a few of the guys once a week to play guitar, but because of conflicting schedules they decided to try a couple of early morning sessions. "Sorry man, I had some things to take care of. They couldn't wait." He didn't offer any kind of explanation; the last thing he wanted to explain was a frolic with his wife. Jim was the sort of fellow who had always felt that what went on in the privacy of a bedroom should stay private.

An older, balding Latino man with a gray moustache yelled toward them. He had been talking on the phone.

"Benson! Amigo, come over here."

Jim turned from his best friend and quickly covered the distance.

"Yes, sir?"

Pedro rolled his eyes, liking the politeness but thinking it unnecessary. "Hector won't be in today. He's got the flu." He turned from Jim and pointed to a big map highlighted in different colors. "I want you to finish up these ditch lines here...here...and along this side of the road. You know which ones?"

"Yeah, I do," he nodded, somewhat in awe at Pedro's speech; there was no trace of an accent in either language.

"Good. Take the kid along. He can run the brush. All right?"

"I'll take care of it."

"Hector has the grease truck over at his place…guess he was pretty sick. I'll get it picked up this morning and meet with you around lunchtime. You'll have to take your truck until then. Is that a problem?"

Jim shook his head while still looking at the map, hands pushed deep into his Carhartt bib coveralls. "Are the machines up there?"

Pedro had to turn his head sideways to hear better; Jim had a tendency to be soft spoken. "Sí, at Swinson's."

"You want me to clean up their driveway?"

The guys had a good ol' boy deal with the Swinsons. Hank and Virginia would let the county keep the big equipment on their property and in return the county would grade their short driveway. It was more cost effective than moving the machines to another site.

Pedro held up a hand, pausing the conversation.

"Look," he said, shaking his head. "You know I can't tell you to do that. If you do it, don't get caught."

Jim knew the problem.

"So here is my official position," Pedro continued, looking around to make sure there were no witnesses. "Noooooo…" he said, while nodding his head up and down with a grin.

"Pedro, you should have been a politician," Jim laughed.

He turned to go find the kid when his boss called after him again.

"Go ahead and get a few gallons of fuel for your rig, Jim," Pedro added, pointing up the hill to the fuel pumps.

Jim followed the point and shook his head no. "Yeah, right. That's okay. I'll just stop in town. It's on the way."

Harrison was busy doing next to nothing, leaning against his machine, sipping a cup of coffee. Steam rose, fogging his round-framed glasses and causing him to tip his head forward to look out over the tops of them. He nodded toward Jim as he approached.

"You seen the kid around?" he asked with raised eyebrows.

"Yep." Harrison winked from underneath his John Deere hat and tossed his head to the side toward the truck across from them.

Jim backed up a step and looked underneath. Harry was having the young man grease the undercarriage. Jim looked back at his friend, crinkling his eyes; the two of them went out of their way to make the boy's life miserable. Today was a good day; usually Harry would make him do something like this in the rain.

"You under that truck, boy?" Jim barked, trying to keep a straight face.

"Yes, sir!" was the immediate response.

"Well quit layin' around and get a field box and put 'er in Old Blue. Yer workin' with me today." Harrison had to walk away for a second; it was just too much fun.

Jim followed with a big grin.

"And two stacks of cones, boy! And don't take all day; we've got work to do!"

They watched the skinny blond-haired kid with oversized teeth scamper out of the dirt and run across the lot.

"He's a good kid, that one."

Jim nodded. "Yeah, he is. Damn good worker."

"You gonna move your truck closer? Them boxes ain't light." Harrison asked the question knowing full well the answer.

"I should, but damn, I gotta to go to the can, and when you gotta to go, you gotta to go."

"Well, you go, girl!"

Jim gave him the finger with a smile and turned toward the bathroom, though he had to laugh at how silly the words had sounded in Harry's deep gravelly voice.

"Hell of a morning, isn't it, Dan?"

"Red sky in the morning, sailors take warning."

"Hah! Red sky in the mornin', sailors go whorin', my pappy would say."

The kid sorta grinned, still embarrassed from breaking the coffee cup that had fallen out of the truck when the door opened.

Jim sensed it and added, "You're gonna operate the brush today, Daniel. You think you can do that?" He liked the sound of the boy's name; it was the same as his kid brother's.

Chapter One

Danny brightened up. For the most part, all he ever did was labor, even though he had been checked out through on-the-job training for some of the equipment. "I can do it. Yes, sir."

"Good."

The boy wanted to make light conversation, but he didn't know Jim all that well. Most of the time, he was Harrison's grunt.

"You see that 'Millionaire' show last night? That guy almost made it."

Jim shook his head. "No. I don't seem to have much time for television, especially this time of year, with the orchard and all."

"You grow apples? Wow, does everybody around here have an orchard?"

The older man grimaced a bit. "Well, we'll see."

Jim didn't want to talk about farming. It wasn't his favorite topic at the moment. Trade restrictions, among other things, were choking the life out of the orchardist; a lot of families were being forced to pull their trees. It was a difficult job with an open market, but working for years on end without compensation made life unbearable.

"Are you having a bad crop or somethin'?" It was an innocent question.

"No," Jim let out, "collectively we grow the best fruit in the world here. It doesn't matter if it's apples or cherries or pears or lumber or the wheat that's growing up there on that plateau," he added with a finger pointing toward Mansfield. "We're for the most part farmers on this side of the state, Daniel. It's just that a lot of folks in government seem to forget that."

Danny looked away and wished that he hadn't said anything. He hadn't meant to upset his boss.

As the bluegrass music played in the background, Jim steered Old Blue off of the hill and headed down through the small picturesque town of Manson, which was built on the edge of Lake Chelan. Named after Manson Backus in 1911, the north-shore village was a popular destination for visitors looking to escape the madness of city life. They rode past the hardware store, the market, and the post office before rolling into an old gas station.

Jim opened his door to talk with the owner.

"Mornin', mister. How's about a fill-up of the good stuff and a case of oil."

"Sure thing, sunshine. See ya got the kid with ya today."

Jim turned his eyes toward Danny as he spoke. "Yeah, you think it's okay I let him ride up front?"

The station owner laughed, and Jim shut the door to his truck while the boy shook his head. Danny could hear the two talking about some duck that was wandering around the fuel pumps; he directed his attention to the inside of Jim Benson's truck. He was certain that the truck had never been cleaned. Not that there was any garbage or anything, just dust, lots of dust. Mixed in were shotgun shells, cassette tapes, fishing lures, a can of Copenhagen and a few books.

Dan picked one entitled *The Teaching of Buddha* and opened it to a page that had already been folded. It read:

"Once a beautiful and well dressed woman visited a house. The master of the house asked her who she was; and she replied that she was the goddess of wealth. The master of the house was delighted and so treated her nicely.

Soon after another woman appeared who was ugly looking and poorly dressed. The master asked who she was and the woman replied that she was the goddess of poverty. The master was frightened and tried to drive her out of the house, but the woman refused to depart, saying, 'The goddess of wealth is my sister. There is an agreement between us that we are never to live separately; if you chase me out, she is to go with me.' Sure enough, as soon as the ugly woman went out, the other woman disappeared.

Birth goes with death. Fortune goes with misfortune. Bad things follow good things. Men should realize this. Foolish people dread misfortune and strive after good fortune, but those who seek Enlightenment must transcend both of them and be free of worldly attachments."

The kid's face turned sour. "That don't make no sense," he muttered, returning the book to the dash.

As the truck left the station and began its journey through the maze of apple orchards, the boy spoke up.

"How come you read all this kinda stuff?"

"Stuff?"

"That Buddha book," Danny said, pointing to it.

Jim, caught a little off guard, raised his hands off of the wheel a bit. "Harry loaned it to me. Why?"

"Well, it's kinda weird ifn' you ask me, and it ain't very Christian like neither."

"What did you read in there to give you that idea?"

"All that talk about goddesses and stuff. There's only one God, and his name is Jesus Christ."

"Well, that's your opinion, young man—not that I'm disputing you. It's just that there are a lot of others in the world who would."

"They're wrong."

"Well, I'm glad you've settled all of the world's creation problems," Jim added with a smile. "Thank you. We'll have all of these other books burned, with your approval, of course."

Danny grinned. "Make it so."

Jim let out a deep sigh. "Look," he said, his tone turning serious, "most of these books have got somethin' to say—so don't be so defensive over your ideas and treat everything as a threat—you could be wrong."

They rode the rest of the way in silence.

"El Dorado," Jim said, stopping the vehicle in front of a large gated deer fence. "It means land of abundance."

"No, it means I get to run machines instead of a shovel," Danny thought as he jumped from the truck to open the gate.

Chapter One

The big red rigs sat behind a manmade boundary, separating the green orchards from the brown desert. Rocky hills dotted with golden grass and purple sage shot up the slopes away from the fences, their smell dominating the air. To the west unfolded one of the deepest and most pristine bodies of water in North America, Lake Chelan. Jim paused for a moment as he got out of the vehicle, taking it all in.

"Snow will be comin' soon."

Danny followed Jim's eyes to the highest peak in the range of mountains that defended the lake, Stormy Mountain, which loomed some fifty-seven hundred feet above the water. He knew the old man was right, but wasn't ready for the long cold winters they endured, at least not yet. Right now he spent his off time fishing for bass on one of the smaller lakes when he wasn't out hunting quail with his dogs. The time would come for snowmobiling and skiing and ice fishing. He just wasn't eager for it.

"Ready, kid?"

"Oh, yeah, let me at it!" Dan replied with a huge grin.

"Good. Now get the grease gun out and give 'em a good goin' over."

"Yes, sir!" Dan added with a salute and jumped into the back of the truck to dig through the field box.

Jim checked fluid levels and gave the machines a quick inspection, looking for loose or worn parts. When they were through, the equipment was started and left to warm up.

"Hop in the front, boy!" Jim said while sitting himself down on the pickup's tailgate. "Drive us up around that blind corner and I'll set us out some cones."

Danny's mouth dropped open. He was going to actually get to drive Old Blue, the oldest, crappiest truck in town.

"Cool, " he thought.

"Come on now. Don't stand there with yer mouth hanging open. Git to it."

Danny didn't have to be told twice, and in a puff of blue smoke, the truck rattled up the road.

With other helpers, the job would certainly have taken longer, but Danny was a natural with equipment, almost as if it were an extension of his body. Harrison had recognized the talent right away; it was another reason why he was so fond of young Daniel.

They pulled back inside the gate, shutting down the noise.

"Whew! It's gettin' hot!" Jim complained, pulling off his bibs.

Danny nodded back as he drank from a water bottle, spilling some water onto his dusty white tee shirt. He couldn't help but notice Jim's "guns," what he liked to call biceps. Jim was the sort of guy Dan called "armed and dangerous."

"You lift weights?"

"Yep."

"A lot?"

"When I can. There's no excuse for not exercising. Having a body that works well is worth a few minutes of sweat."

Danny nodded back in agreement.

The ringing of a phone drew their attention.

"Jim Benson."

"Hi, honey! Am I catching you at a bad time?" It was Mary.

"Nooo. No time's bad to talk with you, sweetie. What's up?"

"I wanted to remind you about the open house at the elementary school tonight. The kids are really counting on you being there."

"Oh, sure. When?"

"It starts at seven."

"Okay. I've got to get some spray on those trees, but I guess I can finish it up when we get back. Say, if you get a chance, call John and ask him if he got a lead on any good pickers. Would ya do that for me?"

"Yes. Where are you?"

"Lower Joe Creek Road…just got finished up."

"Well, okay, I won't keep you. I love you."

"I love you, too, Mare. Bye."

"Well," Jim said, looking at his watch after tossing the phone onto his coveralls, "let's go up an' get those cones picked up, then we'll have us a little lunch. Sound okay?"

The boy jumped into the driver's seat of the pickup again, this time without having to be told.

"Just go up past 'em, Danny, and we'll catch 'em on the way down."

The kid looked up into the rearview mirror and nodded back. Jim watched the cones go by, enjoying the ride while his feet dangled just inches above the blacktop. He couldn't help but take notice of the valley again, especially now, since harvest was his favorite time of year. Jim always did like the cool nights and warm days. He remembered the visitors from Russia who once said to him, "We didn't know that such a most beautiful place on earth existed."

It was a big deal when they came. Jim had even volunteered to have a big Manson-style barbecue at the house, the kind where half the town showed up. He remembered overhearing a conversation that day. Mary was inside at the kitchen table and had just finished doing one of the older Russian ladies' fingernails. His wife was always doing something like that for somebody else. She just liked people. The old woman reached out and put both of her hands around Mary's and began to babble away in Russian without blinking her eyes. There was another woman who understood bits and pieces of the language, just enough to convey the meaning.

"She's talking about the nail polish, and all of the different colors that you have." Mary watched the old woman, taken by her seriousness. "She wants to know why. Why, Mary, is it that you have so much, and she has so little?"

Chapter One

Jim thought that Mary was about to cry. It was easy to get lost in your own problems in small-town USA, and even easier to forget just how really fortunate you are to be an American. Mary made sure that when the woman left, she was able to hide in her things the nail polish, all that she had.

"This is a good life I have been given, a good life indeed," Jim said to no one in particular, as the truck made its way upward.

High up on a hill, Jim noticed a man on horseback just as the Chevy made its turn back down the road. Though the stranger was too far away to identify, he guessed that he knew him because the man raised a hand, so Jim waved back.

"Hell of a hill to be riding on," Jim muttered to himself.

"Not so damn fast, boy! Slow 'er down," he called. The squeaking of dusty brakes filled the air with a pow-pow-pow of engine backfire.

Jim tucked three of his fingers in the stake hole of the bed for balance and leaned out with his right hand to catch the first cone. He swung back hard to toss the cone behind him, dropping it in the greasy plywood-covered bed with a thump. He liked hooking cones. The next one came, and with precision he snatched it from its resting-place, flipping it beside the first one.

Rattlesnakes make a very distinctive sound, and Jim heard one hidden somewhere in the rocks, disturbed by the ditch cleaning. His eyes searched for it in vain, almost missing the next cone.

"Oh, damn," he had to laugh, but managed to grab it anyway. It would be a little embarrassing for him to have to tell the kid to stop and back up.

Jim stretched out and turned around to see how many more there were, but had trouble seeing because of the sharpness of the corner. The noise from the brakes of his pickup seemed louder than it should have been, and he became mesmerized by the spinning tire. Then he realized that the sound wasn't coming from his vehicle at all; it was behind him.

His head whipped around in horror, but it was too late. The apple-hauling rig was traveling way too fast for the load it was carrying, and smashed into the back of Old Blue, pushing it sideways and off of a slight embankment. Strapping snapped, releasing the apple bins and sending thousands of Red Delicious apples crashing and rolling in all directions.

The big truck squealed and slid, its poor brakes doing little to slow it down. The driver panicked and over-corrected, causing the vehicle to tip on its side, where it slid off of the road and into the new ditch. Gasoline gurgled from its tank and disappeared into the dry dirt. In a matter of seconds, it was over.

Plumes of desert dust swirled into the air while apples raced each other down the steep road. Wheels spun and men bled. In years to come, some of that fruit would grow into trees as a living memorial to the accident.

Chapter One

Not more than a minute or two later, a red county pickup came up around the corner and stopped just below the overturned truck. It was Pedro. On the other side of the hill, a man and a horse were in full gallop, moving as one straight down the mountain, on an incline so steep that it would be difficult to walk. Few men whose boots have met the stirrups could perform such a feat. The man's skill was only matched by the surefootedness of the animal.

"YAW!" he cried while spurring the Palomino downward. The straw cowboy hat left the man's head and settled upon the greasewood. Hard pounding of earth changed to the metallic clicking of asphalt while they raced onward. As the cowboy cleared the corner to an unfolding nightmare, he pulled back hard on the reigns, making his horse slide to a stop. For a brief moment he did nothing.

"DISPATCH 911. WHAT IS THE NATURE OF YOUR EMERGENCY PLEASE?"

With measured words, the man responded, "Roger, Dispatch, this is Pedro Mendoza from the County Shed. Say, it looks like an apple hauler turned over on its side. It's in the ditch and we've got apples from hell to breakfast up here. Can you get us some traffic support, a wrecker and maybe a medic? I'm not yet sure if anyone is hurt."

"MR. MENDOZA, WHAT IS YOUR LOCATION?"

"Dispatch, we are at Lower Joe Creek Road, about a mile or so up from the Wapato Lake Road." He paused, noticing the orange traffic cones still standing as a warning. They pulled him in, causing him to wonder at their order amidst such chaos.

"MR. MENDOZA? ARE YOU STILL THERE, SIR?"

All of a sudden it dawned on him what may have happened. Pedro leaned as far forward as he could, pressing his face against the windshield, trying to see up the road. He sat frozen in disbelief, staring at the crushed back end of Old Blue.

As his door swung open, he began to scream into the cellular phone, "I NEED HELP UP HERE, NOW!!!!" and raced toward his friends.

Wheezing in terror, he made his way to the wreck, the phone still repeating the same question. Pedro looked inside the driver's window to find young Daniel slumped against the steering wheel. He reached for a pulse and the boy jerked awake. Danny was bleeding from a cut on his forehead.

"MR. MENDOZA? TELL ME HOW MANY PEOPLE ARE INJURED." The phone talked to nobody. "MR. MENDOZA? MR. MENDOZA? ARE YOU THERE, SIR?"

He raised the phone to his ear. "Stand by, Dispatch."

Although he was out of breath and his hands were shaking, Pedro managed to pull out a handkerchief from his pocket and put it on the boy's face. "Here, Daniel. Hold this to your face. You're going to be all right."

Chapter One

"What? What?" Danny looked around, unsure of what was happening. "What's goin' on? Mr. Mendoza? What's..." The pieces were beginning to fit together.

"You've been in an accident. You..." his voice trailed off as his attention turned toward a loud noise in the direction of the apple truck. A man was climbing out of the window and jumping to the ground. He looked around and then ran toward the orchard, fleeing the scene. Pedro's attention shot back to the boy's screams.

"JIM!!! WHERE IS JIM??"

Startled, the older man looked around; there was a saddled horse in the middle of the road, watching him. Where had it come from? Panic began to set in as the boy continued to scream.

"JIM WAS IN THE BACK! WHERE IS HE?!? PEDRO, WHERE IS HE?"

Mendoza let go of the boy and sprinted up the hill toward the road, but the dry desert grass provided little traction for his cowboy boots and he slipped, driving his chin into the ground. Undaunted, he dug his heels in and forced himself upward. The horse neighed and backed away.

Pedro looked up and down the road, trying to find Jim. Time. He was thinking about time. The panic of not enough time...wondering how much had gone by?

"MR. MENDOZA, PLEASE RESPOND. HOW MANY ARE INJURED?"

"Oh, no...Jimmy...Oh, sweet Jesus. No..." He made the sign of the cross and kissed his hand. Up the road and in the ditch was Jim Benson, lying face up. A man was bent over him administering first aid. As Pedro got closer, Jimmy began to look more like a prop in a cheap horror movie than the man he knew. Three of the fingers on his left hand were missing and his right leg was mostly torn off, lying at an unnatural angle to his body. Jim's eyes were wide and unmoving, as if they were frozen. Other than the slow gasps for air, he was motionless.

The cowboy had already undone his own belt and applied it as a tourniquet to the leg. This stranger moved with precise, methodical movements that could only be learned through practice.

Pedro knew this was bad, really bad. Jimmy's blood covered the cowboy's hands and fancy blue western shirt. Pedro could only watch as the stranger pulled hard on the shirt, exploding black onyx buttons into the air. Then, removing the clothing, he wrapped it around Jim's mutilated hand and searched for further injuries.

His friend was dying. Mendoza just stood in the middle of the road staring, seeing everything move in some kind of terrible slow motion, and it was causing him to feel dizzy. For a moment, he couldn't hear anything but his own heart beating. Something brushed up against him. It was the boy.

"Oh, God. No...Jim...No...Jiiimmmmm!" Tears and blood poured down his cheeks. "I didn't see him. I didn't see him." He fell into the ditch beside the big man whose black hair now darkly outlined his pasty white face.

Chapter One

"Hold this, kid!"

The sharp tone of the cowboy's voice calmed Danny down, and he grabbed the now red shirt and squeezed, though his blubbering continued.

"MR. MENDOZA? THIS IS 911 DISPATCH. PLEASE RESPOND."

The cowboy whirled around. "Give me the phone," he said, taking a few steps out of the ditch to take it from Pedro.

"911, my name is Mat Prose. We have a male, approximately forty years of age, who has suffered multiple traumas. His right leg has been severed just below the patella. I have applied a tourniquet; please note the time. The victim is also missing three of his left manual digits. We are applying direct pressure and treating for shock. What is the E.T.A. of the rescue squad?

The sounds of the sirens in the distance answered.

"THE RESCUE SQUAD IS EN ROUTE, MR. PROSE, E.T.A. THREE MINUTES."

"Roger, Dispatch." He handed the phone back and leaned in close to his patient.

"Hang in there, Jim. You're gonna be alright. Just hang in there."

Everything told Jim that he was dying, but his mind wasn't thinking about death. Instead, it was reliving a conversation that he had had with his wife last night. Their phone had been ringing...

"Hello?" Jim had answered. Mary was right beside him, already asking who it was. For some reason, wives like to think that their husbands' ears work independently of each other and insist on talking into one of them as soon as they see a phone on the other.

The voice on the other end of the line hesitated for just a moment, then asked, "Does the study of religion lessen your opinion of your fellow man?"

Click. The man hung up. Every so often they would get a strange call like that, with some sort of off-the-wall question that made Jim's mind start working.

"It was one of those again, wasn't it?" she asked with impatience in her voice.

He nodded, hanging up the phone.

"Well? Are you going to tell me?" she asked, tugging on his flannel shirt.

"Yeah, this guy is so weird. Doesn't he have anything better to do than mess with a poor farmer's brain?" Jim told her the message.

"That is weird! At least its not some pervert." Mary wrinkled her nose when she said "pervert."

Jim had shrugged his shoulders and watched his wife for a moment longer.

He could see her now, in his mind, and the air was filled with her smell. She was in the garden, wearing a big oversized straw hat with a wide brim. "Mary," he was calling to her, "Mary, how does your garden grow?" and he started to laugh to himself.

"Okay! Come on now. He's up here!" Pedro and Danny were rolling big wooden red bins labeled MGC out of the way so that the paramedics could get closer, waving the rig on.

The cowboy stayed close to Jim, holding the mutilated hand with his shirt. He started to whisper to the dying man in some strange, eloquent language.

Jim's eyes began to blink open, and although his ears could not understand the syllables, his heart did.

"I am with you, my brother, and we will meet again. I will be with you on your journey."

Jim could see his red blood on the man's brown skin, but he couldn't see his face. Jim wanted to be able to see his face.

A patrol car with flashing lights turned the cowboy's attention up the hill. Help was here; it was all around them.

The older paramedic grabbed his cases and jogged toward Jim, trying not to slip on the crushed apples. "Oh, damn," he said, losing his composure. "It's Jim Benson." Looking into the eyes of the cowboy, he found his strength again and went to work. His voice was somber as he yelled back to the young girl who had come with him.

"We don't have a lot of time. Get Life Line in motion and advise the hospital. Hurry."

She nodded back and ran toward the rig.

The deputy had just finished talking on the radio and made his way down the hill, expecting the worst. He didn't have to look in the ditch to know who it was. He knew by the truck. It was Jim Benson. Mary was his wife's best friend, which made them buddies by default.

He was the one who was going to have to tell her; it was a part of the job that he never wanted to do.

At the same time the medics were working, Mary stopped what she was doing in her garden to take notice of a spray helicopter whirling over an orchard not far away. The earlier siren from the fire station that blared throughout the valley left her with an uneasy feeling— as it always did. When the flying machine banked for another pass, she could see a big man wearing a little white crash helmet. As it spun away, she found herself fidgeting with her little gold cross and staring at a wilted pumpkin vine. Something was wrong. She was sure of it.

Reality now sank in for the first time. The rush was over and they all watched the Life Line helicopter climb back into the sky just beyond the big red road grader. The cowboy sat on the tailgate of Pedro's truck as the helicopter turned west, carrying Jim Benson and his belt away. Another deputy was asking him some questions while filling out a report. One of the firefighters had given him a shirt to wear.

"What is your middle initial, Mr. Prose?"

"U," he answered.

"Do you have some identification, sir?"

Mat pulled out his wallet and handed the officer what he needed.

"I see you're Tribal."

"Yes," he replied, pulling his long black hair back from his face with a certain amount of pride.

"Sir, I need you to tell me everything that you can remember about the accident. Can you do that for me?"

He told the officer what he wanted to know.

When they were done, Mat got up and walked toward his horse, which was gorging itself on apples, unconcerned by any of the activities that had transpired.

"Wetoyes! Those will make you sick. Stop that now."

The horse raised her head and neighed, walking away from the cowboy. He picked up the pace to a slow jog and the animal trotted away even further. Mat stopped. The horse stopped. He put his hands on his hips and cocked his head. The horse neighed.

He pointed a finger at her and said, "We're not going to do this now. Not here."

Wetoyes snorted, raised her head and whipped her tail. She turned away from him and continued up the hill in the direction from which they had come.

"Hey!" he yelled. "I'm not kiddin' around. It'll be the glue factory for you!"

Mat kicked the ground and the chase began. The volunteer firemen watched with dull amusement as the two went off, but it quickly dissolved into concern for their friend.

Chapter Two

Through it all, she sat at his bedside, Mary did, and sometimes she prayed and sometimes she cried, but she never gave up. At first it wasn't so bad; Jim even counted himself as lucky.

"It could have been worse, " he kept telling visitors, and figured that with all of the advances in medical technology, he'd be as good as new—well, except his music.

The loss of his ability to play guitar was what saddened his heart more than anything else. It dawned on him what that old lady had meant. When Jim was a kid, he took piano lessons for a short time. One day, on the way to his lesson, he encountered a group of men moving his teacher's piano into a truck.

"What are you doing?" he protested.

"Make it, rags," one of the younger fellows told him.

"Go on, boy, get out of the way now," another told him.

"NO!" Jim remembered yelling. It was funny now; a little skinny freckle-faced kid picking a fight with this group of men. "You put that back where you found it or I'm gonna tell."

They all stood stone-faced for a moment, then started howling. Jimmy was turning red when a little old woman with white hair and a flowered dress came outside; she was his teacher.

Jimmy looked at her and said, "These fellows are taking our piano. Tell them to put it back!" The men kept laughing at the defiant little one.

"Oh, Jimmy, I'm so sorry. I forgot to call your mother. Come sit with me. We will talk."

Still scowling, he followed her over to a small bench in the yard.

"Jimmy," she said, putting a frail old hand to his shoulder, "these hands," and she held them up for him to see, "can no longer play. They are too old. Do you understand?"

He didn't, but nodded his head yes anyway.

"So in a way, the music has died inside of me, and I must let it go and be content with the memories that it has given me."

Jim's mind raced back through time to his present. "The music," he said out loud, "has died in me." And how he would miss it. Often, after a long summer day, Jim liked to sit out on their deck and play into the darkness. More than once his kids had fallen asleep on the old porch couch while he sang to them.

Chapter Two

His attitude would see him through this, as it had the difficulties of life before. The day he was released from the hospital, friends and neighbors lined his driveway and yard, clapping and cheering and bringing gifts. The people of Manson understood that when it came to meeting the needs of others, they should tend to their own back yard before going someplace else. Whatever adversities Jim faced, they wanted him to know that he wasn't alone. Manson gave him something that he had always looked for in his life, a sense of belonging.

They say bad luck comes in threes. Jim, however, didn't need to wait for number three, because number two finished the job.

On his third night home, another catastrophe hit. As he explained it, Jim had woken up in the night, screaming from a recurring nightmare about the accident. In vain, he tried to dodge the apple truck but only managed to jump out of bed, and without the balance of two legs, he fell, striking his face on the corner of the dresser in their room.

He lost an eye and gained seventy-one very fine stitches across his face.

Jim Benson was never the same from that day forward. Whatever will to overcome he had possessed seemed to have been removed with his eye. As days passed, he became more and more despondent. Mary came home from an errand to find him outside on the deck with a half-empty bottle of whiskey.

"Damn it, Jim! You know you're not supposed to mix alcohol with your medication. It could kill you."

She stared at him in disbelief, wondering how much farther he had to go before he hit bottom.

"Finish the job the truck started," he slurred at her.

"Give me that," she demanded, trying to take it away, but got shoved back for her troubles.

He laughed a gruesome laugh and took another drink. His unshaven whiskers stuck up through the scabs, making his appearance even more grotesque.

She stood staring at him, angry.

"What? Is this the plan, Mary? God's great plan? For me to be like this?"

"Stop it. You're drunk."

"What did I do to deserve this? Huh? Tell me. No…no wait, I'll tell you.   NOTHING!"   he screamed. "I DIDN'T DO ANYTHING!!!"

It was quiet for a while and then he started to laugh.

"Well, there goes that 'work hard and be rewarded' theory, don't it? Hah! What a crock that is. What did I do to deserve this, Mary? Not a Goddamned thing. Nothing. So tell me, why? Why me? Huh?"

She looked away from him. This wasn't her husband. This wasn't the man she had fallen in love with…Her husband didn't know the word "quit."

"What? You don't think I see them? The way they look at me? The way *you* look at me?"

"Is that what this is about? The way they *look* at you? Jim, this whole town stood right beside you through it all. You know that! And what did you give them in return? Huh? You quit. You gave up and you quit on them. That's why they are looking at you, because you're not man enough to stand up and move on."

"I didn't ask you! I didn't ask any of them for their damned help! All right?" He screamed at her, "I should have died that day. Who asked that fool to interfere?"

Mary looked at him for a long moment. "I did," she said, while tears slid down her pink cheeks.

But the tears didn't soften his hatred.

"Oh, so you want me like this? And what did you have to give the devil, Mary? What was it worth to you to have this done to me?"

She moved in closer and slapped his face, hard. Hard enough to cause the stitches to bleed. "LÂCHE!" she hissed at him in French.

"Coward? Maybe so." His voice turned cruel. "Go ahead, Mare, finish the job. I won't even fight back."

"Go to hell, Jim."

"HA HA HA!" He threw his head back. "Been there, done that, and got the face to prove it!"

Mary hadn't moved. She was so tired of all of this.

"Youuuu..." he garbled while struggling to pull himself to a standing position. "You, Mary Benson." The whiskey bottle fell from his grasp and Mary watched it spin away, pouring its contents into the voids of the wood.

"Youuuu," he continued after rolling his one eye back into his head and holding the bandaged hand out towards her, "are the Bride...of Frankenstein's Monster."

She stared back at him, waiting for his theatrics to end. "No," she said flatly, "I'm nothing more than a widowed bride," and went into the house, closing the door on him.

Instead of things getting better in their relationship, they got worse. Jim became more hateful with each passing day. He would turn on anyone who crossed his path, as if he were looking for the absolute bottom of life. One day Mary told him to get out; she wouldn't have him anymore. So he moved away from his family to a small trailer on his parents' land some two hundred miles west.

The Kitsap peninsula, an expanse of land that shoots out into the Puget Sound, was a perfect place for Jim to hide away from the scrutiny of rural living. This was where "opportunity" married "anonymity," and he was more than willing to become their "son."

Here he felt faceless, among the towering evergreens and freeways and people. In public, he was rarely noticed by the masses hurrying themselves from one self-imposed deadline to the next.

His father had retired here, and here he was going to stay. The land that they were on was one of the few isolated blocks remaining, bought well before the big boom and still sought after by developers. Other than Jim's occasional new "friends," who helped him to reinforce his destitution by sharing with him their own, visitors didn't venture past the numerous "no trespassing" signs.

Chapter Two

"You in there?" The old woman held a hand up to the screen as she peered through the door. "Jim? Jim!" Her voice rose to a cackle.

Jim moved a little on the couch, his head pounding from last night's drinking binge.

"Yeah."

"Git off that sofa and unlock this door. I haven't got all day for this nonsense. It's eleven o'clock in the morning! The day's half over and you're still in bed!"

The fact of the matter was that Jim had been up earlier, but had decided to just drink a beer and go back to sleep.

"Do you have to yell so damn loud, Ma? I'm comin' already."

"Don't you swear at me and don't you call me 'Ma.' I don't know who you think you are anymore, but you don't have to call me like I'm some old hillbilly woman."

Jim rolled his eye and got up off the couch, staggering some.

"I've always called you 'Ma,'" he told her while flipping the latch on the door. "Why don't you just reach in through the hole in the screen like everyone else?"

Their eyes met briefly, but Jim swung his head away, letting his long black greasy hair hide what the beard wouldn't. He was trying to remember where he had left his eye patch.

"Oh, for the love of God! Look at this mess," she told him with pursed lips, but her eyes went back to her son. "Jim, you smell. Go in and take a bath." He was disgusting, as usual.

Jim clinched his teeth while she made an exaggerated wave in front of her face as if she were fanning the smell away. He let out a long sigh and started toward the bathroom. Bathing didn't matter to him, not like it did to her; she was the cleanest person he knew. Besides, getting undressed meant having to look at the stump of his leg.

"No, wait!" she added. "There's a basket of clean clothes in the back of the car. You get those first."

Jim turned back around and hobbled out the door. He could smell her perfume.

As he came back in, arms loaded, his mother started in on him.

"Did you call your grandpa today?"

"I just got up!"

"It's his birthday, Jim. The least you could do for that man is to call and wish him a happy birthday. For that matter, you should call your wife, too."

He didn't want to talk about Grandpa or Mary or the kids or Manson or anything else from his old life. He just wanted to be left alone. Arguing with his mother was something else he didn't want to do, so he lied, "I'll call him in a while, all right?"

She seemed pacified. "Fine."

On the way to the bathroom, Jim stopped by the refrigerator and grabbed a beer, despite the cool looks from his mother.

Chapter Two

"What's this?" she screeched while holding up the classified section of the newspaper that had been spread out on the table.

Jim stopped again and dropped his head; she was determined to nag him to death. As the double vision he was experiencing began to fade, he noticed her green slip-on shoes pointing their toes at him. Right away he knew she was wearing a pressed green housedress with brown buttons because she ALWAYS wore that green housedress with those green shoes.

"Now, we've talked about this and talked about this. What's wrong with you? You didn't call on any of these, did you?"

He couldn't remember; he was pretty drunk last night. Circled were those kinds of classified ads promising lots of money and little work, something that appealed to Jim—the easy life. He didn't care if it was the lottery or the sweepstakes or if it came from the handle of a slot machine, as long as it had that guarantee—the one in black and white—"Guaranteed Winner." For him it was an escape, away from what he had become: someone that he hated.

"You are going to do nothing but squander your settlement money, son. This isn't the way to any kind of life. Why do you keep looking for some kind of shortcut?"

Maybe part of him just wanted a way back to Mary. Maybe if he had more money, she would want him back.

"We keep going over this same tired road, Ma. Can't you just leave well enough alone?" Jim was getting angry. He had tried the other life and it landed him here. Couldn't she see that? Couldn't any of them see that? "Will you just stop already?"

"Don't you take that tone with me, James Oliver! You want a good crack? I'll bend you across my knee. As God is my witness, I'll do it."

Jim burst into a quick laugh—his mom was no bigger than Mary was.

"Yeah, I'll just sit over here and be scared for a while."

As he opened the beer in his hand, the phone rang.

"Benson."

"Mr. Benson? Sam Troupe here. We talked last night."

Oh, crap. He did call somebody. His mind was a fog. "Sam?" he couldn't quite put the pieces together.

"From Tacoma. We talked about the Australian Shepherd." The voice spoke in a heavy Texas accent.

Bingo! Jim remembered. "Oh, yeah! Yeah, right." He was trying to act casual so that his mom wouldn't get interested.

"Say, I'm calling to let you know that we were fixin' to leave. As a matter of fact, we should be there in about an hour and a half?"

"Great. Thank you for calling." He hung up the phone just tickled pink. This was it: a foolproof plan— even better than those hundred lotto tickets he had bought with the number one, a secret code for "won." It seemed Sam Troupe was looking to unload a first-class cattle dog, for nothing. *And* it just so happened that the neighbor next door was in need of one first-class cattle dog. Jim would just turn around and sell the animal for a tidy profit. Easy money.

"Who was that?" his mother asked while clanking dirty pots together in the sink.

"Oh, ah...That was the parts store. They ah...got that new pump in for the tractor finally," he lied. "Took 'em long enough." Now he was thinking that if he could only get rid of the old gal for a while, he could pull this off.

"Next thing we've got to do..." The Texan's voice trailed off with no trace of accent. He was looking around for the little dog. Two Eyes peered up from the leg of the dining room table she had been chewing on. As the man continued to speak, her ears went up and down, up and down.

"Next thing we've got to do is get you cleaned up. Pure-bred Australian," he began to laugh. "Hah! Truth is, your momma just wasn't that picky, now was she?"

Two Eyes lost interest in the ranting man and began devouring the leg again.

"Heck, none of your family seemed to be too...Darn it!" he said, jumping to his feet, realizing that the dog was chewing up the table again. But quick as lightning, the mongrel was gone.

"You know that this isn't our stuff and I'm going to have to fix it, don't you?" he called after the dog as he got down on his hands and knees for a closer inspection of the damage. "Oh, for crying out loud, would you look at this. You had better…" He stopped talking in mid-sentence to listen to the noise coming from the living room. It sounded like the dog was tearing something up. He crawled back out, bumping his head on a corner of the table. "Damn."

"I'll save you from the couch monster, stupid man. Die, couch monster, die!" She snarled and growled, her head jerking from side to side. Pieces of fabric and foam flew in all directions from the arm of the sofa.

Sam's face became red and veins began to pop out near his temples as he looked over what was left from the battle of the arm.

"WHAT ARE YOU DOING?" he yelled. "Have you lost your mind?"

The little dog looked up at him with a piece of foam hanging from her mouth. "Oops. Sorry. I was being a dog. It's kind of fun."

"I'll fun you! Get off that couch!"

"Oh, quit being an anthropomorphite," Two Eyes told the short heavyset man with the receding hairline. Then, while putting a back paw to her ear for a little scratch, she advised, "Put a little duct tape on it; it fixes everything."

Sam looked confused. "An anthro…what?" he stuttered, not knowing what the word meant. "I can't use duct tape to fix a couch!"

"Picky, picky, picky."

"You are not going to like the payback for this one.
You've sunk to an all-time low. In all these years I've
never done anything this bad to you, but this is it,
missy. Next it's my turn. You think this is funny, don't
you? You're just laughing it up, right? Well it's not.
No. It's not funny at all, you little...little..."

"Angel?" she interjected. The little dog's head went
from side to side, her ears going up and down, up and
down. "And what did you say? 'Never done anything?'
Lordy! That's a convenient memory. I'll have to get me
one of those. Besides, you're doing it to me right now
with that shirt you're wearing."

"My shirt?" Sam looked down at the short-sleeve
plaid material. "What's wrong with my shirt?"

"It hasn't been in style for thirty years, that's what!"

"But I thought that..."

"That's what you get for thinking," Two Eyes
interrupted.

Sam scowled. "I'll tell you what. It's time for a bath
and a haircut. You've got work to do and it's my job to
make sure you look authentic. Come here, poochey
woochey."

Two Eyes watched the approaching red-faced man.
"In your dreams, old one," she mocked before
beginning her escape.

His hair was still wet from the shower as Jim sat in
the living room fiddling with the artificial leg.

"When are you going to go in and get a new leg?" A
question she asked him almost every visit.

"I dunno," he answered, thinking, "Here we go again." The problem with the leg was that it was only meant to be temporary, more like a trainer leg. What had pissed Jim off so much at first was the fact that it was black. He was a white guy with a fake black leg. The doctor tried to explain that there was some kind of mix-up in shipping, and that everything would get straightened out, but it didn't help Jim's attitude. He used to have plenty to say about having an integrated body, mostly off-color jokes. With time he not only got used to his rather odd-looking partner, but also held a certain fondness for it, even though it wasn't a very good fit and often times left sores.

"You could walk better with a new leg, you know."

"Nag, nag, nag."

She grabbed the newspaper again, folded it in half and whacked him across the head.

"Ow! For Christ's sake, Ma, you don't have to…"

Whack! Whack!

"Don't you take the Lord's name in vain and quit callin' me 'Ma'!"

He used his sleeve to wipe away the beer that had spilled on the couch, shaking his head.

"Your father never talks to me that way. Why do you do it?"

"Oh, Ma, why do you have to bring him into the conversation every damn time? Huh? The man hates me; it's that simple. I live less than a block away from him and he doesn't so much as even stop by once in a while to see how his crippled son is doing. I'll bet he drives for four hours to go see *her*, doesn't he?"

"Of course he does. He loves Mary."

"I'm the son here, not the son-in-law—the son! She is the daughter-*in-law*, not the daughter. Get it?"

"You know how he feels. He told you."

"He told me once. We got in the Chevy and we went for a ride and he told me all right. I haven't seen him since."

"If you would just quit this nonsense and decide to go back home, I'm sure he'd be the first person in line to drive you."

"I didn't leave! For the nine-zillionth time, she threw *me* out!! Why do you keep saying I left?"

"Why do you keep telling yourself that you didn't?"

The conversation was progressing exactly as it did every time she came over. Jim took a big drink of beer.

"Honey, why don't you come to Mass with me tomorrow? You'll feel better."

"No, Ma, I won't." Something in the tone of Jim's voice had changed, and the way he spoke just now was more distant than his mother had ever heard. "I won't go, ever. You don't understand this, I know, because you're one of them—the Believers. I'm not."

"Oh," she said, coming closer and wringing her hands together, her voice concerned. "Don't talk that way—not to me."

He closed his eye but kept on talking. "I'm on the other side. I'm like the kid who just found out that there is no Santa Claus, that there is no Easter Bunny,

Mom...I know there is no God." Jim opened his eye again, a sad eye. "But you go ahead and believe the dream; I won't stop you. Just don't make me part of it, okay?"

"No, no..." She knelt down beside him and put her hand on his. "God is real, Jim. You've just closed your heart to Him and it shows in your life. Listen—"

But he cut her off. "No, I will not. I didn't close my heart. I prayed for help, and for my trouble I lost an eye. You're the only one I've ever told this to: I didn't fall that night in a dream like I told everyone. I was getting out of bed to pray on my knee. You tell me why God would take a man's eye for praying."

She was shocked and couldn't for the life of her answer him.

"I'm not alone either. There are a lot of us who know the truth, who aren't blind anymore. We don't want anything, except to be left apart from your rituals and your guilt. Darwin was right. We're nothing more than animals."

Jim's mother just patted his arm, listening.

"I wish...I wish my life could be different, Ma. I really do."

Eager to go, Two Eyes had jumped into the front seat of the Cadillac. "Visiting" was her favorite thing to do.

She spent most of the trip bouncing between the front seat and the back window of the Texan's car, when she wasn't insisting on trying to drive, of course.

"Get off me, you retard!" the Texan ordered, but it didn't do any good. She would either give him an ear lick or just try to crawl between his legs to help with the pedals.

She loved to go for rides, but not nearly as much as she loved to be left alone in the car. There was always such good stuff to eat: a left over French fry, a crumb off of a sandwich, a headrest. Once the Texan had come back to find that every inch of every window had been licked by the funny-looking dog with smelly breath. It had made his whole car stink.

Sam stopped the car to double-check the directions and Two Eyes gave him a quick lick.

"Oh, would you stop it already!" He was still upset about the furniture, but upset or not, Two Eyes loved him.

"I dunno. Maybe I wrote down the directions wrong. This place doesn't look right," he mused, looking the situation over.

The little dog jumped up, putting her paws on the dash and tilting her head to the side, her ears going up and down as he spoke. "Smells right to me."

"It doesn't make sense. Over here," he said pointing, "we've got these fine fences and cattle, but he lives in that run-down trailer?" Sam looked at the dog for reassurance, but of course got no help, because Two Eyes was thinking she had died and gone to heaven.

"Why would he pay so much attention to the corrals and so little to his own place?" He shook his head while looking at the directions again. "I dunno, dog. If this is it, it kinda sucks." A part of him was feeling a little bad about having to leave her here. "But then again," he said with a grin, "so do you!"

The dog fell back into the seat as Sam mashed down on the gas pedal, steering the big red car toward the trailer.

After gassing the engine a couple of times to keep it from dieseling, Sam turned the key off and got out of the car.

"Howdy!" he drawled toward the black-haired man. "You must be Jim Benson," he said, offering his hand. "My name is Sam Troupe. It's a real pleasure to meet you."

Jim nodded back, agitated that the Texan had shown up early. Now he'd have to explain this to his mother. There was also something familiar about the man that he couldn't quite put his finger on. Jim was certain that he had never laid eyes on him before, but something else kept saying that he had.

"Beautiful day, isn't it?"

"If you say so," Jim let out with a grumble. "That the dog?"

"Why yes, sir, it is, and if I might say…" He was cut short by Jim's approach, and he backed up as the bearded man hobbled toward him.

The Texan stared down at the leg.

"Now I don't mean to be too nosey, sir, but is thar somethin' wrong with yer leg?"

"Damn Texans anyway," Jim thought.

"No, *thar* ain't somethin' wrong with it. It just ain't *thar*," he said sarcastically.

Jim opened the door and Two Eyes jumped into his arms, giving her famous: "let-me-lick-the-inside-of-your-mouth-because-there-might-be-something-left-over" greeting.

He peeled the animal's head back and held it in a grip that caused her to quit struggling. Peering into the dog's eyes he said, "This is an ugly dog. This is the ugliest dog I have ever seen. If you look up ugly in the dictionary there would be a picture of this dog."

The Texan couldn't help but grin because he couldn't agree more. Jim set the dog down, and to his amazement she just sat there looking up at him, her head going from side to side, her ears going up and down, up and down. Jim was wondering who was checking out whom.

Then, as if things weren't strange enough, it appeared to Jim that the little dog turned toward the Texan and winked. His fantasy was interrupted as Two Eyes bolted toward the Herefords.

"Well?" Jim asked, glaring at the visitor.

"Mister, anybody who wears a belt buckle as fine as that," the Texan said, pointing at Jim's, "has got to be all right."

Jim glanced down at the buckle he was wearing. It was the belt that the cowboy from the accident had used as a tourniquet. No one was ever able to find out who the mysterious Mat U. Prose really was, because none of the police reports checked out. The buckle had been won at the Suicide Race in Omak, a very long time ago. None of the old-timers would give him any kind of a straight answer, just something about the greatest rider the hill had ever seen. Jim had mixed emotions about the mystery man. He didn't know if he wanted to thank him or kill him, because sometimes Jim wished that he had been left alone to die. Either way, he always wore the bloodstained leather belt and buckle. The Texan had a strange look on his face, like he was waiting for Jim to figure something out. It was in his eyes; Jim knew he had seen those eyes before, but where?

"The dog is yours!" the Texan said, holding out a hand to shake. Normally Jim wouldn't have, but the strangeness of the man overpowered him. As he reached for it, he realized that the Texan was, again, holding out the wrong hand. He was left-handed, and the bearded man switched hands, letting the Texan grasp his chopped up appendage.

Mr. Troupe, noticing that there were fingers missing, asked, "Ah, you a cabinet maker?"

Jim jerked his hand back, pissed. He mocked him back. "No, ah, you an idiot?" and grumbled some more unpleasantness. He was just about to really lay into the guy when the car door slammed shut and the Caddy left as quick as it had come.

Vulgar words were shouted from within the house as the little dog flew past Jim through the hole in the screen door. Jim winced at the sound of his mother's voice and went inside.

Chapter Two

"Never in my…" she said, looking down at the dog. "What in the Sam Hill is that?"

Two Eyes sat at her feet, looking back and doing the ear routine. The dog loved the smell of this new house and decided to give it her personal stamp of approval. Jim's mother watched without expression as the dog squatted and peed in the middle of the carpet.

Jim fumbled for words. "Uh…" Come to think of it, he didn't even know the dog's name.

"Well?"

He hobbled over to the refrigerator for another beer and she followed him with her "look." Jim knew that look, too, and thought about blowing it off when he remembered rule #2: "Never blow off Ma's look."

"That is what I'm gonna sell to the moron next door," he laughed. "The road got his other dog last week, boo-hoo, and this is just what he needs, a real cattle dog."

He popped the top of the beer open and added, "That puppy there is worth five thousand dollars."

"Five thousand dollars? Did they amputate your brain, son? Cattle dog, smattle dog! That dog is no more of a herd dog than that cat," she screeched, pointing an old finger toward Nine Lives.

"Cat?" Two Eyes thought. "Did somebody say 'cat'?" She threw her nose into the air to find the furry-faced critter. "Ah-ha!" she exclaimed to herself after spying the hunched-up hissing ball of orange.

"Oh, for crying out loud," Jim's mother bellowed, but it was too late. Two Eyes was in a dead run to meet her new roommate.

"Cat mouths are my most favorite thing to lick," she thought.

The greetings were concluded as the can of beer exploded on the wall just between the two rivals, sending each of them, terrified, in different directions. Jim hobbled back to the fridge for another beer.

"Damn, none left," he grumbled. "I'm goin' to the store. Ma, you want somethin'?"

"No," she answered, "and quit callin' me 'Ma'!"

Two Eyes was searching around the room. "Where there's cats, there's gotta be…Bingo! The jackpot, the mother lode of mother lodes…the litter box!"

"Oh, no you don't!" The woman was quicker than the mongrel, and pulled her back by the little blue collar.

Jim stood loading his lip with Copenhagen, wondering how that dog could even think about putting that in her mouth.

"Come on, SFB," he barked. "Let's go for a ride."

"Ride?" The psycho dog bolted for the hole again, leaping over the porch and into the yard.

Mrs. Benson crossed her arms with more disapproving looks; Jim hadn't bothered to renew his driver's license and went out the door pretending not to notice.

"Don't you open any of that beer on the way home, Jim."

"Nag, nag, nag."

"If they catch you one more time you'll spend time in jail. Are you listening to me?"

Jim rolled the eye again and headed for New Old Blue. While he was in the hospital the first time, Harry and the guys at work had repaired his truck, complete with a new engine and paint job.

"Git in, dawg, an' don't go and eat nuthin' that ain't yours."

Two Eyes jumped to the seat while spinning circles and barking. As Jim got in, he stomped on the gas pedal three times, hollering in between each stomp, "There's no place like home. There's no place like home. There's no place like home."

Chuckling to himself, he noticed the little dog staring at a bumper sticker stuck on the glove box, which Jim had tried to tear off. It read:

Be i f fu w h your
arate school
f   w

"Damn Harry and his Kung Fu stuff anyway," he said with a grim expression.

Jim pulled the shift lever down and the rig slid out of the gravel driveway in a cloud of dust. Two Eyes looked out the back window at the old woman standing beside the screen door with her arms crossed.

"Good-bye Auntie Em," the dog thought. "We're off to see the wizard."

Jim was just letting off the gas pedal as they approached the stop sign. He was looking around the dash for a banjo tape when the dog leapt between his legs after a half-eaten apple on the floor. Jim looked down with a few choice curse words, missing the stop, and when he looked back up, he saw the face of death, White Freightliner.

The big rig was moving 20 over the 30 mph speed limit. It hit the tail end of the Chevy so hard that it separated the cab from the bed, leaving the two pieces in ditches on opposite sides of the road before jackknifing and flipping. The scraping and sliding came to a sudden stop, and only one thing could be heard in the peculiar silence, Old Blue's radio.

"Good-bye, Mary. Good-bye, Jane. Will we ever meet again?"

The wreck was over half a mile from the house, but the old woman had heard it, and went to find what was left of her son.

"E-block, can you hold?"

"No, it won't wait. This is an emergency. Get my husband, now."

"Yes, ma'am," an apologetic voice responded.

Moment's later, Chief Benson's words echoed across the phone lines. "What's wrong, Janey?"

"Jimmy's been in another accident. This one's bad, Jack." She started to cry into the phone when she said his name. "They want to move him to Chelsea. It's his head; he's unconscious."

Chapter Two

"Where are you?"

"I'm at the dispensary. They need our permission to move him."

"I'm on my way. You just hold on. I'll be right there."

The metallic blue '66 Malibu screeched sideways into a lined parking space. A rather large man in a cook's uniform jumped out and ran to the lone woman. She collapsed in his arms, bellowing.

"He's gone. You're too late. He's already gone."

"What?" The strength in her legs and the color in the man's face were both draining away. He was afraid to ask again. "Where? What do you mean, gone? Gone where?"

"Oh, I'm sorry. You thought..."

"Yeah, for a minute I thought that he had died."

"I wanted to wait for you, but they said it had to be now."

"Did he ever wake up?"

"Only when he was getting sick, and then his eyes would roll back in his head. They said he could be in a coma."

Everything that Mr. Benson had heard so far made him think that his son was done for. Jimmy was so accident-prone, and a part of him always knew that something like this was bound happen.

"Okay, look, we need to get moving. The other hospital is a couple of hours away. Did you call Jenny yet?"

Mrs. Benson shook her head no and pulled a worn Kleenex to her nose. Mr. Benson thought she looked on the verge of a breakdown.

"Go call," he urged, thinking that having something to do might help her keep her sanity. "I'm gonna get directions and talk with the doctor if I can. Go on now."

He watched her as she toe-trotted away, the way a cheerleader might. Mr. Benson, still following her no longer visible footsteps with his eyes, seemed unwilling to proceed. He was thinking to himself how yesterday, though it was so many yesterdays ago, he had stood in a similar place, waiting for God and her to bring their son into the world. Now he wondered with sadness if God wanted Jim back, and asked Him to wait just a little longer.

Neat as a pin, Jim Benson was tucked into a hospital bed in a darkened room. Something caused him to jump awake, as if someone had thrown cold water in his face. His head was pounding so hard that it was difficult for him to think. The smell—hospital smell—it brought back so many painful memories.

"Hi, honey."

He knew that voice; it was his mother's. She was there with him again. She was always there, no matter how hard he tried to make her go away. The room was very quiet. Jimmy reached out with his good hand and touched her; her skin was as soft as ever. Over by the window he could see an orange glow. Camels. It was his father, but why was he smoking again, and in a hospital of all places?

"Is Mary here?"

"Mary? Who's Mary, honey?" Jim's mom looked across the room toward her husband, but Mr. Benson didn't have to see her face to know that she was worried. He could tell just by the tone of her voice.

Jimmy became suspicious. What the hell was she talking about?

"Do I stutter? Is my wife here? Has she bothered to show up? I notice he has." Jimmy motioned with his head toward the old man. "For him to show up things have gotta be pretty damn bad, right? So what did God want back this time? Huh? Let's do an inventory, shall we? WHAT DO YOU SAY, HUH?" His voice rose to a scream. "LET'S FIND OUT WHAT'S NOT BEHIND CURTIAN NUMBER ONE!"

Jim's father, without moving a muscle, clicked on the lamp beside him and everything in the room appeared.

"MOTHER FU..." Jimmy blurted, but couldn't quite finish the phrase. What his eyes were telling him now wasn't real. It couldn't be. He was in another dream; it was the only thing that made any sense.

"Son?" Mr. Benson's throaty, smoke-laden voice was concerned yet stern.

Jimmy rotated his head toward his father; he was so...young. The old man's face reflected his son's terror, but he had also seen something else in the boy's eyes, just for a moment: hatred.

Since the accident when he had lost his leg, there wasn't a day that had gone by that Jim Benson hadn't wished to start his life over—to be a young boy again with the promise of a full life ahead—but this was different. This was too real, like that stupid cat dream he used to have. His attention turned back to the sheet pulled across him. Somehow he knew what was underneath and his wiggling toes testified to it. Putting his hands to his face, he could feel fingers, all of them. The sensations had caused him to quit breathing for a second. But what dominated his thoughts was the ability to see again; his depth perception was back.

"Son? Are you all right?" Mr. Benson asked again, halfway closing his right eye.

Jimmy just nodded back, not knowing what to say. He turned his attention toward his mother, just as a man walked into the room.

"Well, look who's awake." The doctor locked eyes with Mrs. Benson for a moment before sitting down beside the boy.

"My name is Doctor Baum. Do you know where you are, Jimmy?" the man asked, looking over the top of his black-framed glasses.

"I'm at Chelsea Naval Hospital, in Boston," Jim replied, but he didn't look at the doctor, rather at the captain's insignia on his lapel.

"You remembered. Good. Now tell me, young man, why are you here?"

"I had another accident at school and was brought here by ambulance last night," he said, though he couldn't believe that the words came from his mouth. Jim felt as if he were a mere spectator, watching the scene unfold from a distance. The truth was that this had happened to him when he was fifteen, but how he remembered the details escaped him. Besides, none of that mattered. What he wanted to know was how he got here.

"Hmmm. What day is today?"

"Saturday," he answered to the warm quiet lull of the man's voice.

"Where do you live, Jim?"

"On Shore Road, in Cape Neddick." That sounded so foreign to Jim, but familiar none the less, to be back in Maine.

"Uh-huh. Do you have any brothers or sisters?"

"Two sisters and a brother."

"How old are they?"

"Let's see, ah, Jenny is seventeen, then me, then Danny who is ten and little Sarah is six," he answered with confidence, but the feeling of being an observer to all of this remained.

Doctor Baum glanced toward Jane Benson, to see if she contradicted anything. She gave him a nod. Jim noticed it; he also noticed how stiff the man appeared, like he was uncomfortable about being in the room.

"Where's your dad work, Jimmy?"

"He's in the Navy. He's a cook."

"Probably a pretty good one, too, huh?"

"Yeah."

"What's the date?"

"June somethin'," he shrugged. "Twenty O...ah, nineteen seventy one."

The brow of the doctor briefly wrinkled at the slip of speech. He pulled a penlight out of his pocket and leaned toward Jim, looking into his eyes.

"Hmmm, how's your head feel?"

"Sore, like a headache or something. I was a little disorientated for a minute, but I think I'm okay, just tired, and hungry."

Hungry. That was the word the man in the white coat had wanted to hear. But Jimmy knew that; he knew everything that was going to happen. As a boy he wouldn't eat the hospital food, and it was that fact that had kept him overnight for additional observation.

"Good. You should be. You threw up for two hours. Remember anything about it?"

Jimmy shrugged again. "Bits and pieces is all. Guess I got whacked pretty good."

"Yeah, you sure did. Okay, look. We're going to get some food in you, see how well you hold it down, and maybe run a few tests. If you do all right, we'll talk about sending you home later today. Fair enough?"

"Yes, sir."

"Polite young man. I want to talk to your parents out in the hall for a while. A nurse will be in shortly."

"He," the little baldheaded doctor said, while taking off his glasses and rubbing the bridge of his nose, "seems to be out of the woods, for right now anyway. Jim has retained both long- and short-term memory, which frankly surprises me a little. Normally with an injury this severe, there is at least a temporary loss of short-term memory. What I'm seeing and what my experience tells me don't mesh with one another. So, I don't want to get your hopes up, considering that I don't have any good medical evidence to support my hunch. Now, did you notice anything out of the ordinary about his behavior or any of his answers?"

Jim's mom looked at her husband, not wanting to speak up first, but she did. "Well, he was asking for his," she hesitated, feeling somewhat foolish, "his wife. Someone named Mary."

"He was also very angry for a brief moment. I just assumed that he was disorientated," Mr. Benson added.

"Uh-huh. When you say angry, tell me what went on."

Jim's father cleared his throat. "When I turned on the light, he looked right at me and yelled Mother F..."

"Oh, he didn't say it, Jack," Mrs. Benson interrupted with a swat towards her husband. "He almost said it, but it wasn't like he said it."

"He meant it, Jane. You know that boy meant it. Have you ever heard him use that tone or that kind of language? I haven't, and to be honest it was more than a little unnerving."

She nodded in agreement.

The doctor let out a deep breath. "Let's not get all worked up over this. Like I said, it's almost a miracle recovery. Oftentimes a patient's behavior can be a little bizarre when they first wake up, almost like they are still in a dream. I'll check his progress in an hour." He gave them a quick smile and started to walk away, but then stopped and asked, "His wife?"

Both of the parents nodded.

"Huh, that's a new one for a kid."

Addled by his new circumstances, Jimmy lay in his bed, looking at the ceiling. Though he couldn't comprehend how he had come to be in these surroundings, he was all too aware of their ramifications and he started to shake. It's one thing to wish for something, but it's another to actually get it. Now all he wanted to do was just wake up in his crappy little trailer.

"You okay, honey?" his mother asked while sitting back down in the green chair by his bed. She was holding her mouth rather funny; it told him she was nervous. Then it dawned on him: She wasn't wearing her red lipstick. He had NEVER seen his mother leave the house without it.

"Yeah, Ma, I'm fine." But you are so weird looking, he thought. You look like a kid. My mom was always old.

Mr. Benson stood over them at the end of the bed, holding onto a fresh cigarette with his index finger looped over the top of it. Jim felt dwarfed by his presence. The old man looked tired, he thought, with dark circles under his eyes. This must be hard on him. It made Jim wonder why he still felt angry. After all, his father hadn't done anything yet. What had he said that day in the car? The longer he watched his father, the clearer the memory became.

"Listen to me, son," he had told him. "A man carries a lot of burdens on his shoulders as he goes through life. It doesn't matter who you are, either. Sometimes that weight bears down on your soul so hard that you just start to crumble. There are two things in my life that have given me the strength to see those few moments through. One was God, and the other was my family. When I see you now, the way you are, crumbling out here away from everybody, I don't hold it against you for your decisions. Rather, I hold it against myself, for not teaching you how to bear it. I thought that I had through my example."

Looking back, Jim realized that it wasn't his father he was mad at. He was really mad at himself, for letting his father down. Mr. Benson was a warm, giving man who never seemed to talk a whole lot, as if he had trouble expressing himself.

"Son?" Jim's father asked, using his free hand to scratch his flat-top haircut. This was one of the ways Jim always saw his father in his mind when he thought of him. One hand on the cigarette with a finger looped over it, his forearm tattoos prominently showing, and the other hand scratching the top of his flat-top haircut.

"Yeah?" But his voice cracked a little, the way some fifteen-year-old boys' voices do.

"Are you sure you are feeling okay?"

"Yeah, Pap, I'm okay. I'm glad that you're here," he whispered.

"Where else would I be?"

Jimmy knew that the old guy would walk through the fires of hell for him. How could he have treated him so badly?

The boy's eyes drifted away from his father, and now he was looking at his mother, much the way that one might contemplate a painting on a wall. His feelings of being just an observer were going away, leaving him with little doubt that this was real. Jim *was* fifteen again. It should have overjoyed him, to get what he had always wanted, but it didn't. Maybe he was just stuck in the great circle of want—wanting any other life than the one he possessed. Maybe it was worse than that. Maybe his ignorance had led him to believe that by being young again, everything in his life would be easy.

Over the course of the ensuing hours, young Jim Benson was subjected to every medical test conceivable in 1971, including something called an EEG that involved wires stuck to his scalp with needles, only this time he didn't scream during the procedure.

His parents were talking out in the hall with a different doctor. Jim wasn't sure why, since he could hear every word they said.

"Well," the doctor was saying, "he seems to check out. Have you noticed anything out of the ordinary in his behavior today?"

Chapter Two

"Jim seems quiet to me," his mom answered.

"Oh, he's probably just tired, honey. I know I would be."

The doctor nodded in agreement. "Well, I'm going to discharge him. There is no reason to keep him any longer. Let me be very clear though: Jimmy was unconscious for eighteen hours, long enough for us to begin deliberating the possibility of surgery."

Mr. Benson stiffened at the prospect.

"All of our tests indicate normal brain function; however, I want you to keep a close eye on him for the next few days. Watch for abnormalities, especially violent behavior. If there is anything that you need to talk about, you can call me, or visit the dispensary in Portsmouth. He's a lucky young man, and most likely he will be just fine."

"Thank you, doctor," they both said in unison.

Jim breathed a sigh of relief—at least he was over this hurdle. Emulating the normal behavior of a fifteen-year-old was his next obstacle. Jim wasn't a kid anymore; how was he supposed to behave like one?

Though he had fooled the doctors, he couldn't fool himself. Jim wasn't "just fine" and still couldn't figure out how he had been moved through time. "Why would I wake up here, of all places—the hospital? Am I sick?" The last thing he could remember was his mother coming over to the house. After that, nothing.

Other pieces of his life however, were falling into place with perfect clarity. Something he hadn't experienced in a long time. This was another pressing question. Why? Was it this youthful body? Perhaps. The lack of alcohol in his system? Doubtful, because even sober Jim knew what poor decisions he had made. Then it dawned on him. It was hatred; he had been blinded so long by hate that it prevented him from thinking very clearly. Now that he had his body back, the desire to inflict his misery upon anyone who came near him had left him. Left him or not, though, he wasn't happy—not like he had envisioned. In fact, he felt depressed.

Jim Benson had gotten what he wanted all along: the opportunity to start over. What could be so wrong with getting what you want? Then it hit him. What if this wasn't his life at all? If it had been a repeat of his life, he shouldn't have been able to change anything, because if it changed, even just a little, it wouldn't be his. If every event in his life, good or bad, was built upon something else, changing it would have caused a different outcome. He had wished to go too far back in time. There would be no way to follow steps that he couldn't possibly remember, and he had already changed this life by getting out of the hospital a day early. Then another reality struck him. Fate wasn't to blame for his life, but rather his reactions to the situations life presented him.

Now, as Jim sank down into the hospital bed, he understood the horrible reality. Even if he could somehow manage to find Mary, the chance of ever seeing his children born was very slim. Somehow, in the course of just a few short hours, Jim Benson had destroyed everything in his life that had once meant something to him. No matter how low he had managed to drag himself, a part of him always knew that he could go home to her. Now that wasn't even possible. "Always" didn't have nearly the permanence that he had assumed.

"Well, Tiger," his father said with a manufactured grin as he came in the room, "it's time to get going. Let's get you dressed."

Jim didn't have to be told twice. He was up and pulling on his pants. If he stayed in the bed any longer, he was sure that he would go mad.

"It'll be good to get you home."

"Yeah, it will. Seems like it's been forever."

"Here you go," his father said, handing Jim his shoes.

"Where's Mom?"

"She's down the hall, at the nurses' station."

Jim sprang to his feet, somewhat astonished at how supple his new-old body was.

"Let's go, kid." Mr. Benson put an arm around his son to guide him down the black-and-white tiled hallway.

A few steps out of the room, Jim's head started to spin. The anxiety wouldn't leave him alone.

"Pap," he started, but the words sounded to him like they were coming from somebody else. "I'm gonna use the bathroom before we leave."

"Oh, good idea. It's a long drive. I'll be right down there," his dad said pointing to the desk where his mother was standing.

But Jim couldn't see it. "Okay," he said, and turned to go back into his room. The boy crashed unnoticed into the side of the doorjamb before making it back into his room. A song that kept playing in his head over and over again grew louder with every step. Jim wanted to scream and tried to hold his hands to his ears to block it out:

"Good-bye, stranger. It's been nice. Hope you find your paradise…"

He staggered toward the bathroom, grabbing onto anything that might support his weight. "Oh, Christ, what's wrong with me?"

The boy was thankful that the door was open and the lid to the toilet was up, otherwise he wouldn't have made it.

Wreeetch. Jim began to throw up. "This isn't what I wanted. This isn't where I'm supposed to be."

"They say the devil is my savior, but I don't pay no heed."

"Oh, my God." Wreeetch. He fell back against the puke-green colored wall, trying to stay off of the floor. He waited for the room to come back into focus and the music in his head subside. Jim turned away from the toilet, only to see his reflection in the mirror above the sink.

"Son of a…" Jimmy whispered while wiping some of the vomit away from his mouth, still not used to seeing the skinny boy with shoulder-length hair staring back at him. He turned on the water and splashed some of it onto his face, cleaning himself up.

"Who are you?" he mumbled to the reflection.

Jim straightened the room up as best he could and made his way out and down the hall toward his parents before anyone became suspicious.

Chapter Three

"Wake up. Everything is beautiful."

Something stunk. Jim opened his eyes and jerked backwards. Little Sarah was giving him a good look-over just inches from his face, singing to him with last night's milk breath. Her hair was in little blond tangles, complete with a booger stuck to her nose.

"In its own way. Bomp." She pushed a finger on his head. "Does your owie hurt?"

Jim tried to pull away but the wall beside his bed prevented it. She asked the question again while creeping even closer, forcing Jim to cover his nose in self-defense.

Thinking for a second about the question and looking into her blue eyes, he answered, "I'm fine, little girl." But he was wondering if they had changed color as she grew older. "Is it time to get up or somethin'?"

"Mommy sez it's time to get up and see Jesus," she answered, still poking on his head.

Jimmy rolled over and buried his face into the pillow. "Now I know I'm in hell," he thought. "It's Sunday and we're Catholic."

Sarah mistook his gesture for play and jumped on him.

After his little sister had finally left him alone, Jim sat up in his bed and studied the room. There were so many things here that he had forgotten, things that he once cherished. Though he recognized them, they for the most part had lost their significance—it was just kids' stuff now.

Extending his feet over the side of the bed, Jim hesitated before setting them down on the freshly waxed hardwood floors that ran throughout the home. They were meticulous, just like everything else in the house. There was little doubt: Jane Benson was a "working" mother.

After his shower, Jim stood contemplating the face in the mirror again, still asking himself if any of this could really be happening, when the thoughts were interrupted by his mother's voice.

"Jenny, Jimmy, Danny, Sarah, breakfast."

There was a tap at the door.

"Immie, Mom sez time to eat."

"Okay," he answered, opening the door. "Thank you," he replied to the little girl. All of the Benson children had brown eyes and jet-black hair, except Sarah. The family joke was that the milkman had once visited, but the truth was that two of Jim's aunts were twins and also blue-eyed blondes. Another peculiar thing about his little sister, now that he thought about it, was that she never called their father "Pappy" like everyone else; she always called him "Daddy." It must be why his father always referred to her as his "Daddy's girl." But then everything was peculiar to Jim—his whole family. "I don't know any of them anymore," he said aloud. "Or at least I don't know any of them yet."

During "Breakfast with the Bensons," Jim began to feel pretty sure that no one knew his secret. The red Formica table with metal legs sat against the windows, just inside the kitchen door. The kitchen was large, with white cabinets, white walls and red trim that his mom had painted to match her favorite table. In a way, it made him think of Mary's kitchen, so neat and ordered, with plenty of colored glass jars filled with pastas and beans adorning the countertops.

He could tell that they were all a little apprehensive, because they were asking him some of the same questions that they did last night. Nervous chatter, his mom would have called it, and he looked at her, grinning at the thought. Having a family member almost die causes certain disruption in relationships, though Jim doubted that anyone except his parents understood the severity of the accident.

Mr. Benson added new flavor to the conversation. "Well, Grandma and Grandpa should be here this afternoon."

The statement brought a smile to everyone's face except Jim's—it had caught him off guard. The look of surprise on his face didn't go unnoticed as he thought, and it was his mother who made a mental note; her husband's parents had been planning this trip for over six months.

"But it's been exactly one hour and sixteen minutes!"

"I don't care how long it's been," Jenny told Danny with clenched teeth as they walked through the doors of the church. "If you don't quit timing everything I'm gonna take that away from you."

Danny scowled back at his big sister, shaking the oversized gold colored watch on his wrist at her. "Pappy gave it to me, and I'll tell."

"Shhh." It was mom.

Danny made a face at his sister anyway and stuck out his tongue.

Jim was the last in line, dawdling along, still trying to get a grip on his new surroundings. Without thinking, he reached out to put his hand into the holy water just inside the door, but as he realized what he was doing, he jerked his hand back as if the water were fire.

"No," he said, though it wasn't audible.

He continued following the family toward their customary spot, pausing so that each of them could go down on one knee in the aisle and make the sign of the cross upon themselves before sitting down.

"Spectacles, testicles, wallet and WATCH," Danny blurted out while making the sign of the cross.

SMACK! Went Jenny's hand up alongside her little brother's head. Then she pointed at him while he slithered into the pew.

Jim touched a quick knee and scooted in beside them. As soon as they were all seated, Mr. Benson pulled down the knee rest and Jim watched as the family knelt again and began to pray.

Exasperated, he copied their motions, but didn't pray like his family—or anyone else in the church for that matter.

Instead, he thought, "I believed in You my entire life, and I saw what You did to me, what You did to my family. You did not show Your love for me, only Your contempt. I did nothing to deserve such harsh judgment. There is nothing that I want from You. There is nothing I ever want to say to You. Just leave me alone. My life this time will be better without You." Jim sat back up into the pew well ahead of anyone else.

While they waited for the service to begin, bells from the church tower rang, causing an instant silence throughout the congregation. Jim's father had gotten up to talk with some of the other men in the room, and when he came back, Jim noticed that his face was solemn. The older man bent his head toward his wife, and when they were done whispering, Jim followed his mother's glance across the church to another family who seemed to wear his father's same expression. Something was wrong.

There was a little bit of commotion in the front of the church just before the music began to play. Everyone stood up as the priest entered. It was Father O'Brien, dressed in purple liturgical vestments. Jim knew that all of the colors meant something, but it been a long time since he had attended a Catholic Mass, much less thought about the apparel.

The priest was a little old man from Ireland who had white hair and a brisk walk. Mr. Benson always summarized the priest with two words, "He cared." There was usually some stranger helping out around the church, doing odd jobs, someone who had run across a bad patch in his or her life and was down and out. Father O'Brien was the rock for these people. He made sure that they had a dry place to sleep and warm food in their bellies, without preaching or judging. Jim's father had once told him that the priest would buy an occasional bus ticket out of his own meager salary to send them home when the time came. When they asked how they should repay him, his standard answer was, "Whenever, never, forever, whatever."

The priest waited to let the hushed whispers quiet themselves before beginning to speak to them in a beautiful Irish accent.

"I was looking over the bills of the church this past week. I saw"—though with his Irish accent it sounded like "sar"—"the phone bill, and the light bill and the bill from the hardware store and such. And I was thinking to myself how important it was to keep paid up, to not fall behind. It is easy to fall behind, because no matter how much you have, there is always something else that comes along and wants the money. It may be a broken hot water tank, or a new lawn mower, but it is always something."

Jim noticed that there were more than a few people nodding along.

"And you know, it occurred to me, it's that way with God, too. Not to be paid up, mind you, but to *keep prayed up!* Even myself, as I hurry through my day, trying to get this done or trying to get that done, I sometimes forget to just stop and thank the Lord for what a wonderful life He has given me. Oh, it would be easy to put off a simple prayer for something like that, or for the food He has given me. I could even wait until Sunday and get all prayed up at once."

O'Brien paused long enough for the message to sink in, then tilted his head back a bit more.

"But there is one thing about this life that I can assure you: You never know when it is going to end. And for myself, I prefer keeping current with the Lord, if you get my meaning. And another thing: Sometimes if you wait too long, it is easy to feel like you're obligated somehow to the Lord, and maybe you might even try to avoid him, like you would somebody else that you owe.

Remember this, though: Jesus Christ is forgiveness. It is as simple as that. If you have strayed a bit too far from God in your life, Jesus is here with you now, and through Him, all things are possible."

"Fool," Jimmy thought.

"Now if you will all join me in prayer."

Jim bowed his head, and though he heard the words, they carried no meaning.

"Hey, Jenny? Would you come over here please?" Mr.Benson asked while grinding a cigarette butt into the lawn with his shiny pull-on shoe.

"Yeah?"

"You know that boy over there?" he asked, motioning with his head across the street to a family just getting into a station wagon. Both Jim and his mom followed the motion; it was the same family that he had been looking at in church.

"Which one?"

"The oldest."

"Oh, yeah, he's a senior. His name is Paul. Why?"

His father didn't answer. He just told everyone to get into the car; it was time to go. As the Malibu warmed up, he lit another Camel, lost in thought. All of the windows were rolled down, complete with Benson elbows hanging out as the car cruised away from York toward home. They had driven for a while before their father spoke.

"I was talking with Paul's dad," he said. "Paul has been drafted into the Army. He leaves on Monday for boot camp, then to Vietnam." The old man threw the butt of the cigarette out the window as he finished his sentence.

Jim thought he was going to get sick again. His brain went into overdrive. "This had to be a joke, right? Vietnam? Hell, it's nineteen seventy-one. Isn't *that* over with? And what's with Paul? He's only a kid, for crying out loud!"

He turned his head out the window, nauseous, but somehow found the strength to overcome the sensation. The thoughts gave rise to the feeling that Jim had been wrong about his childhood—that maybe it wasn't so perfect after all. He had forgotten what it was like to be fifteen with a war raging on, and now he remembered that there were plenty of nights when he had lain in his bed awake, wondering when his turn to leave would come.

The Chevrolet rumbled along Shore Road, past the ocean, and Jim saw that the tide was going out, leaving everything exposed.

"You goin' down to the beach?" Danny questioned his older brother while stuffing the last of a peanut butter and jelly sandwich into his mouth. The Bensons' house was only three hundred yards off a wooded trail away from the Atlantic Ocean.

Jim shrugged a little, considering that it was a pretty nice day to go exploring.

"You always go to the beach after church," he said with his usual know-it-all tone. "You go to that rock and talk to yourself."

"Rock?" Jim wondered. "What was he talking about?" Then he remembered it, The God Rock.

"No," he said with distaste. "I'm not going." Never, thinking to himself, will I waste my time there again. When Jim was a kid he used to go stand on a very strange-shaped rock that overlooked the Cape's shoreline and talk to God. He called it his God Rock, but he never thought anybody else knew about it.

"Yes, you will. You always go," Danny retorted, as he got up to put his plate into the portable dishwasher.

Jim just watched his little brother walk away, shaking the watch on his wrist.

Never say never. As sure as Danny had spoken the words, Jim stood some twenty minutes later staring at the rock by way of a narrow, winding path that had led him from his house through the dense Maine woods. Besides leading to its intended destination, the trail also led to hidden ponds and secret overnight camping spots, and gave rise to the occasional glimpse of porcupines and fox.

"Kiss my ass," he said, and walked around the rock toward a towering cliff called Bald Head. "When I was a child I spoke like a child, and now that I am a man I put childish things behind me. Get behind me, rock." He turned, picking up a small stone, and threw it toward the platform. "I told you to leave me alone!"

Anger quickened his stride and obscenities filled his mouth, the rigorous climb up the steep trail doing little to soften his anger. Sweaty from the warm, breezeless

June day, Jim paced back and forth along the edge of the cliff, hands on his hips, screaming.

"WHY? Why are you in my head? Get away from me!" Jimmy kicked small rocks and sticks over the edge, where they tumbled and spiraled a hundred feet toward the crashing waves below.

"You son of a…"

FLASH!

Jim saw a bright blue light inside of his head, cutting off the sentence and causing his hands to drop by his side; for a moment he couldn't move. He staggered dangerously close to the broken fringes of earth that once met the sea, unaware of what was happening. Then the sensation stopped and the pain was gone from him.

As his attention focused back, he noticed that the line separating life from death for him was but inches away; yet instead of fear, it brought to him a strange calmness.

Motionless, he stood staring down, thinking how tired of all of this he was, and how it was *he* and not God who was in charge of this body. He could kill it if he wanted to, and there was nothing that God could do to stop him.

"I can get even with You, right now. I can destroy this body You feel is such a precious gift."

The waves continued the hypnotic effect and his thoughts gave rise to power. He felt as if he could fly.

"It's been such a long time," he mumbled. "This was all just a long time ago, and now I'm back, in the twilight zone."

The stillness of his movements, caressed by a new gentle breeze, cooled his sweat-laden forehead. A song came to his lips and he began to sing in a quiet, childish voice.

"A long, long time ago...I can still remember how that music used to make me smile. And I knew if I had my chance, that I could make those people dance and maybe they'd be happy for a while..."

But his words were sounding less like singing now and more like a monotone death chant. *"But February made me shiver, with every paper I'd deliver. Bad news on the doorstep; I couldn't take one more step."* But he was thinking that he could—just one more step—and make all of this go away, forever.

"I can't remember if I cried, when I read about his widowed bride..."

"No," she had said flatly. *"I'm nothing more than a widowed bride."* Mary's words echoed after him, chasing him through time.

Jim took a shortened breath and held it, tears falling down his cheeks while he raised his hands out to his sides. "Let go, Jim. Let go," he could hear in his head. He started to laugh a little. "I can smell bread. Why do the dead smell bread?"

Then his expression changed to a cold stare. "And what does it take to soften a man's heart so filled with hate? Death. It is the answer to everything." Jimmy closed his eyes and whispered, "Oh, Mary, I'm so sorry, my wife. Forgive me for losing you," and began to lean forward.

"MEOOOOW!"

The sound snapped the trance and Jimmy staggered backwards, falling onto the ground. Dirt stuck to his wet arms and face as he rolled from side to side, crying and shaking.

"Meow. Meow," the calico cat spoke, coming closer and rubbing against him. He stared in disbelief as it curled around his leg and lay down between them, blinking gold-colored eyes.

It was the dream coming forth into a new twisted reality. Jim rested his head on the dirt, listening to the animal's purrs, and fell asleep, exhausted.

After ten minutes or so, Jim awoke to the faint sound of guitar music floating across the air. He rolled over and listened for a while, staring at a cloudless pale blue sky, wondering how long he had been asleep. It occurred to him that it didn't matter in the least. Nothing really mattered anymore because he was as lost in this life as he was in the old life. Sitting up, he used his vantage point to determine the direction of the music. It was coming from his beach. The smell of the salt air further softened his anger, and with curiosity he looked around to find the non-existent feline.

"Probably just a damn dream anyway."

For the first time it hit him: He was back on one of the most interesting and beautiful shorelines in New

England. From where he stood there was no end to the Atlantic Ocean; its deep blue color rolled out away from him into eternity. Seagulls dove from the cliffs, soaring in circles before landing upon the seaweed beds below. The trees and rather flat ground behind him gave the feeling that he was alone, as it concealed the summer beach cabins that would soon be filled with occupants. Jim had spent much of his childhood here, and being back made him wonder why he had ever left.

Carefully, the boy made his way back down the steep trail, unsure why caution was now a concern. Perhaps, he debated, the taking of your own life demonstrates supreme authority, whereas losing your life in an unfortunate accident gives rise to the possibility that somebody else may hold the puppet strings.

The guitar sounds disappeared as he jumped down into an eight-foot-wide tideway. Young Jimmy paused for a moment, trying to think what was so special about this spot. He knew that when the tide was high it protected the entrance to the trail up the cliff, but there was something else—he was sure of it. Jim wandered down the seaweed-covered channel toward the sea, sometimes stopping to examine the strange forms of life clinging to the sides. As he progressed, the sheer rock walls shot higher above his head to the point where there was no way out except the way that he had come. The sound of the waves crashing grew louder, reminding him that this could be a very dangerous place to be if the conditions weren't just perfect, as they were now. Deep pools began to emerge and his feet negotiated the pitfalls, but when he stopped, the memory became clearer.

Jim started breathing faster. In his mind, he could see himself lying in the seaweed, trying to dislodge something that he had found in one of the pools. "CRASH!" A strong wave had made its way up the tideway, disrupting the still pool's surface, filling it with white bubbling foam and drenching him. He had gotten up and moved as fast as he could back out. Drowning was nothing a sailor's son would ever want, and he knew all too well how stingy the sea was with second chances. But another wave, this one stronger, caught up with the boy and slammed him down onto the rocks. Before he could make it to his feet another and yet another pounded his frail frame without mercy, driving him into the depths of the deep pool.

He was going to drown, but instead of panicking, he began to pray. As he did, the waters calmed, allowing Jim to escape.

"It was a coincidence, nothing more," he argued and abandoned the memory, turning to leave.

"Man!" Jim let out under his breath. "Why there, of all places?"

His sisters sat perched on top of the God Rock, neither of them noticing his approach.

"That's good, sweetie, but not so high this time. Sing a little lower," Jenny said while lowering her voice a bit. "Now wait for the chord change before you start."

"Okay," Sarah responded, transfixed by the guitar.

"Everything is beautiful, in it's own way," she bellowed at the top of her lungs. " Oh! Hi, Jimmy."

Jenny had to turn almost all the way around to see her kid brother, and when she did, her face went sour.

"What happened to you?"

"Huh?"

"Why's your hair like that?"

"Like what?"

"In a ponytail."

"Oh. I dunno." Jim had had long hair most of his life, and during college he got in the habit of wearing it with a rubber band.

"And you're all dirty."

"I climbed up the cliff."

"Mom better not catch you doing that again. It's dangerous."

"Yeah? Well Pappy better not catch you bouncing those things around without a bra on either."

Jenny might have covered up her conspicuous nipples but something in the way Jim had spoken made her mad, so instead she glared at him.

Jim was thinking that there had to be a rule in here somewhere—maybe something about not pissing off your PMS sister with regard to girl stuff, especially because she was bigger and could easily kick the crud out of her scrawny little brother.

"The day's comin', sis."

"That day ain't today. Mind your own beeswax."

Chapter Three

Jim shrugged, giving in like a married man, and climbed up onto the platform with them. "Let me give it a try," he asked, holding a hand out for the guitar.

Jenny watched him for a second longer, squinted her eyes then lifted the strap over her head, handing the instrument upwards. His sister was the eternal hippie chick. Jenny Benson was extremely intelligent, had a flawless complexion and wonderful sense of humor. The last time he remembered seeing her as an adult, she was still wearing similar embroidered jeans with sandals, and of course, beads. She still gave out her handmade bead necklaces as Christmas presents.

Jim strummed slowly down the strings. The sensation reawakened within him a feeling he had abandoned: love. God, how he loved to play, to make these sounds, to be able to be who he was again. "I'm back," he thought, and in this sense, Jim was now free again. A thousand songs raced through his head, but his fingers picked up where his mind had left off.

"Now do you believe in the book of love and do you have faith in God above, if the Bible tells you so?" he bellowed at the top of his lungs, surprising Jenny.

"Now do you believe in rock-n-roll? Can music save your mortal soul? And can you teach me how to dance, real slow?"

"Whewhoo!" Jenny yelled, clapping her hands together.

"Well I know that you're in love with him, 'cause I saw ya dancing in the gym; you both kicked off your shoes. Man I dig those rhythm and blues..."

"Grandpa and Grandma are here!" Danny hollered as loud as he could from the end of the trail.

Jim stopped playing, feeling an odd sense of excitement. Sarah leapt to her tiny feet and scampered down the rock towards home.

"Not bad, little brother. You've been practicing!"

"Not bad indeed," he thought to himself, considering that it had been almost two years since he played last.

"You still are a little slow on the changes though. Remember how I showed you how to put your thumb on the back of the neck?"

"Yeah." He just grinned; she had always been a better musician, taking after their father in that respect. Jim wanted to play as well as they could, but even with lots of practice, he couldn't begin to have the ability that came to them effortlessly.

"Where'd you learn that song? It sounds pretty good."

"Uh. Just heard it. It's all I know," he lied. Jim didn't know if the song had even made it off the album yet.

She let the comment slide, even though it didn't make any sense to her. Besides, she was almost as excited to see her grandparents as her little sister was.

"Everything is beautiful, in its own way" Sarah warbled.

"That's a real pretty song, honey," Grandma said while setting the last of the silverware on the dining room table.

"Shhhh," the little girl told her. "It's a surprise."

"Well, I won't tell anyone. You can count on me."

Jim watched from his father's chair in the family room, disinterested in the four channels their black and white television had to offer. He got a brilliant idea—so bold that it made him giddy: He could go find Mary. It didn't matter that she hadn't moved to Cape Neddick yet. What mattered was that he knew where she lived and could just jump in the car and go see her. He started to laugh at the thoughts in his head. "Hi, Mary. I'm Jim Benson, your husband. Well, your husband to be. So, ya wanna jump in the back seat with me?" He kept laughing, picturing the look on her face.

"I'll just drive up to…to…" but Jim couldn't for the life of him remember the name of the town Mary grew up in.

"Huh, that's funny. Oh, well, I'll think of it."

There was a knock on the front door.

"Well, come on in, Father. I'm glad you could make it after all," said his mother.

Jim rolled his eyes and sank back into the chair. Even though he liked the priest, he had had enough of religion for one day.

They were all seated around a large rectangular table, decked out with Mom's best linen, china and silver, holding hands with heads bowed. The Irishman paused in silence before saying the grace.

"Dear Lord, I am now reminded of the words of Ralph Emerson. In a book of essays, he once said 'Into every intelligence there is a door which is never closed, through which the creator passes.' I believe he is right about that. As I sit with this loving family of God, in appreciation of their generosity, I thank You, Lord, for reminding us that no matter how far a man strays, he always has the ability to come home to You. Thank you also, Lord, for this truly wonderful family and for the food that we are about to share. In the name of the Father, the Son and the Holy Spirit, Amen."

In unison the family all repeated "Amen." Everyone, except Jim.

Anger rose inside of Jim again, disapproving of the manner in which his family had just groveled. "God didn't provide this meal. My old man worked his ass off for it. If you want to thank anybody it should be him, you foolish priest," he thought.

"Say there, James?" Father O'Brien asked.

Jimmy jumped, briefly concerned that his thoughts had been read.

"Yes, Father?"

With a wink, the handsome man in the rag wool sweater asked, "Would you mind passing me the spuds there?"

"Oh. Of course," Jimmy replied, handing them to him with a bit of relief in his voice.

As the dinner conversation progressed, so did Jim's irritation. The priest kept using the phrase "Good Catholic" to the point where the boy just dropped his utensils on his plate in exasperation. The noisy clank drew everyone's attention.

"You meant to say a 'Cradle Catholic,' didn't you, Ben? Not necessarily a 'Good One,' just as long as they follow the church blindly and attend regularly, with, of course, that oh-so-important tithing. After all, the only thing the church needs is quantity, right? Who gives a rat's ass how ridiculous the doctrine becomes!"

"WHACK!" went Grandpa's hand against Jim's head.

"Ow! Son of a..."

"WHACK!" Father O'Brien smacked the other side.

"Damn it!" Jim yelled, jumping up from the table.

Mr. Benson jumped up as well, but he was taking off his belt.

"Jack, NO!" his mother protested, "and don't hit him in the head anymore! He just got out of the hospital!" She turned her attention toward the older men, and they all dropped their heads in shame.

"Sit down, Jack. You too, Jim."

They did as they were told, unwilling to look her in the eyes; they burned hotter than the candles before them.

"Well, this is a fine Sunday dinner," she screeched, throwing her napkin down on the table. "You had better explain yourself right now, son."

Jim had to remind himself that he was just fifteen, and if he wanted to see sixteen, he had better cool it.

"Sorry, Ma. I don't know what got into me just now. Sorry, Father. I didn't mean to say those things or call you 'Ben.' I was wrong," he said without raising his eyes from his plate.

The silence at his shocking behavior still filled the room.

After an uncomfortable minute had passed, the priest spoke up to everyone. "You know," he said in that same singsong voice, "I sometimes think to myself about the emphasis that is put on winning, and for the longest time I never understood why. I mean, you win or you lose, what is the difference? Really, life goes on.

"I had to look at myself and how it was that I managed to get by, to get things done. Because, as you know, it is easy to fail at something, even if you give it your all. I think that there is something inside of all of us, that just plain wants to fail, as near as I can figure anyway. That part of us comes out and makes excuses for us, the kind that we can live with, so that we don't have to finish what we start. And so, that is what winning is, stopping the part of us that wants to fail, and getting on to see things through."

Taking a sip of red wine, he continued, "I haven't been in the States here for all that terribly long, you know. And I suppose it would have been easier for me to stay at home, because it is a difficult thing to leave your homeland, but staying would mean I would have to see more of the killing. Lord knows I've seen enough of that. You speak out against the Church, James, like we were the enemy, but I'm here to tell you: I've heard your words before and know of the bloodshed that goes along with it. I'm talking about the Catholics and the Protestants back in Ireland. I'm sure you've heard at least something.

"I wouldn't stay and be part of it anymore—not that I was, mind you, but this collar here makes it so. You understand me, don't you? That there are those out there who do not believe in the freedom of religion? I'm going to tell you how I see it, and you can judge it for yourself. You seem to be man enough to do that.

"God made laws for man to follow, to keep him on the straight and narrow. Except man makes his excuses about why he shouldn't have to follow them. Says it doesn't make sense or that it doesn't matter or that the Church is to blame because it won't change with the times. I'm saying that man wants to fail God.

"Some will use the good name of the Church to fight with, the way they justify it to themselves back home, but it doesn't matter because it all comes down to the same thing: right and wrong. Do you catch my meaning here, lad? You can attack the Church if you need too. Lord knows it has always been done. You'll be wrong in doing it, because it is just an excuse for you to believe. Your fight is with yourself, and by trying to tell yourself that it isn't, you just end up hurting the innocent.

"Believe me when I tell you this, James, it is the innocent who do get hurt, no matter what you might think. If you don't believe me, lad, look into the eyes of your mother; you'll see the truth looking back at you."

Jim's eyes wouldn't move from the plate. Shame was overcoming him as the priest paused.

"You can't hear with an angry heart, James. You know what I'm saying. The Holy Spirit is talking to you, all of the time. Don't shut It out of your life."

Chapter Four

"He's wrong," Jim thought as he lay in bed later that night, hearing the words of the priest replaying in his mind. He found himself remembering something that he hadn't thought of in a very long time.

The first time Jim met Mary's mother was on a hot, sticky summer's day, two weeks after he and his new girlfriend had become an item. He had knocked at the front door and stood waiting for what seemed to be an eternity before it opened.

As the door creaked, he turned around, only to be surprised that the woman was seated in a wheelchair.

"Um…is Mary home?"

Marie smiled back while shaking her head, and with a hint of the devil in her voice, answered, "No, she's not. You must be that boy she has been talking about night and day. Jim, I think she told us. Is that right?" Her voice was soothing, like thick warm honey.

Jim blushed. "Yes ma'am."

"Barbara," she said to the older girl coming up behind Marie, "this is Jim, Mary's beau. What do you think?"

"I don't know, Mom," she said, crossing her arms and giving Jim a good slow look over. "Are you sure we've got the right guy? It would be a shame to waste a kiss on the wrong one, even if he's kinda cute."

Jim's face went beet red. Mrs. Actuel nodded and leaned a little closer; she was fumbling with something under a brown afghan that covered her legs.

"Well, you may be right, but I think that he'd be fun to give one to anyway." She motioned with a finger for him to come down closer.

"Crap," he thought. He hadn't even kissed Mary yet.

As Marie opened her hand, revealing a Hershey's Chocolate Kiss, the women started giggling at the obvious look of relief on Jim's face.

Over the next few months, Jim became a close friend with his other "mom," and one day, while he was waiting at the house for Mary, she had talked to him like he was a man. He sat at the kitchen table, noticing how much weaker she had become.

"I want you to hear this from me, the way that I heard it from my mother, because something tells me in my heart that you will always be with my Mary, and I may not."

Jim lay in his bed, troubled by the misplaced memory, knowing that she hadn't lived long enough to see their high school graduations, much less their wedding.

Jimmy had lowered his eyes, but she reached out a chilled hand and touched his to bring him back. "That's what this is about Jim," she said, looking away. "Don't you ever do it."

He could still feel the way she squeezed his hand, and though at the time he hadn't understood, he answered with a simple, "Okay."

"This is the story of my father and it is as true as I can remember it." She let his hand go and leaned back into her wheelchair before continuing. "My father's mother was a poor Protestant girl who lived on the wrong side of the tracks in a little town not so far from here. She fell in love, or maybe just into bed, with a wealthy French Catholic boy who lived on the right side of the tracks. Whatever the case, his father hated her and wouldn't allow her 'filth' to set foot in his house. The old man forbade his son to ever see her. It didn't stop them at first, but when she became pregnant, the father went crazy. So they broke it off and the girl went back to just being poor, only now with a baby boy.

"Things were hard for her. She managed to get a job in a café, where they would let her take home whatever table scraps might be left over, and somehow the two of them made do.

"One day, when my father was five years old, he and his mother were walking to work. They were passing by a big house with a black iron fence and he said that he remembered looking at an old woman working out in the yard. The old woman stopped what she was doing and stared back at him. Suddenly she dropped what was in her hands and came running toward him, screaming his name. It was his grandmother, and, of course, he was the spittin' image of her own son at that age.

"'Jean? Jeanny? My Jeanny!' she cried in a heavy accent, trying to reach out through the bars, tears streaming down her face. Then an old man came out of the house after her and dragged her away kicking and screaming.

"The poor girl never married that boy, but she gave her son his name anyway, Jean LaFollette, and began attending the Catholic Church as well. He told me that his mother once looked at him and said, 'I can't ever give you the money that God knows we need, but I can give you all of the other things that I know you should have had. Jean, I have enough love for you inside of me to make up for him, so you won't ever have to go looking for what isn't there.'

"Well, my father grew up poor, but proud nonetheless. His momma learned to cook, by watching at the café, and when she could, she would bake pies at home. Eventually, my grandmother became the best pie maker anywhere, selling her pies door to door. All baked in a wood cook stove mind you."

Then the other shoe dropped.

"Jim, we have no control over what has been done in our families. What's done is done. We can't run from it, or hide from it, or even pretend that it didn't happen. What we can do, though, is to remember and understand in a way that the mistakes are never repeated. That's all that you can do. No matter what terrible things that you may have thought happened to you or anyone else as a child, you must never pass it on. That's what growing up is. That's what being an adult is.

"You'll remember this, won't you, Jimmy? You'll see to it that my Mary is safe, won't you? I'm trusting you, because I won't be there to do it. We both know that. Promise me. Promise me now that you'll always be there for her and your children and that you won't walk away the way my grandfather did. Promise me now that you will honor her."

She wouldn't let go of his hand until he promised.

Now, Jim pulled the pillow tight to his face to cover his weeping—tears over the crime of a promise broken.

"Oh, God. Mary, where are you?"

Chapter Five

Yawning a bit and stretching, Jim stood alone at the bus stop the next morning, waiting for his ride. As he grew older and looked back, he wondered why he had always called it the "bus stop," because it was nothing more than the end of a common driveway that met Shore Road. With the exception of that road, the driveway and a large adjacent field, he was surrounded by more of the Maine woods.

Jim hadn't slept much the night before. Besides his embarrassing behavior, there was the anxiety that came with the knowledge that he had to attend school for the next three and a half days. It took Jim almost an hour of careful detective work just to find what classes he was supposed to sit in on. He just hoped that he could still find his way around the old place.

"Son of a..." Jim said aloud as his attention focused on the row of crushed mail boxes that were all nailed to a wooden stand. They had been the victim of mailbox baseball again. He walked over to assess the damage—all were damaged except one, that of W. O. Seyte.

"Hmmm, wonder how they missed that one?"

"Not again." It was Danny coming up from behind. "Bet Pappy was ticked off. Really ticked off, especially after what you did at the table last night. Why did you say that?"

Jimmy frowned and put his hands into the little front pockets of his jeans. "Don't know. Wish I hadn't, though."

Danny watched him. "Are you okay? From the hospital?"

This was his kid brother, Jim thought. Always a little more in tune than the rest of the world. He had his mother's eyes, the ones that seemed to look right into you. The ones that could make a stranger feel a little uncomfortable."

"Yeah. Tired maybe, but I'll be fine."

Daniel shook the watch at him. "You've got time."

Jim wondered what he was talking about, when he suddenly got the feeling that somebody was watching them. He spun around, only to find a cat across the street; it was the cat from the cliff.

"You *are* real. I thought maybe you were just a dream or something."

"Who you talking to?"

Jim looked at his little brother. "The cat," he said, pointing. "Is that okay with you?"

The boy followed the point. "What cat?"

"That one," he said with a tone of disgust in his voice, "right there..." But the calico had vanished.

Jim stood open-mouthed for a second. Just then an incredibly old yellow school bus, with an even older driver, squeaked to a stop, blocking his view. For just a second, Jim wondered about the safety of riding with either of them as he climbed aboard and took a seat. His anxiety about returning to ninth grade without attracting too much attention was growing, because Cape Neddick High School was small, and everybody knew everybody else.

Fifteen minutes into the ride, the bus slowed in a shadow-darkened area of the woods and the chatter quieted down enough to hear the click-click-click of the red flashers. A woman stood on the doorstep of a small shack whose roof had been repaired many times. The door to the home was open but it was too dark to see much of anything inside. The old blue housecoat tied tight around her waist was the most noticeable thing about her—that and the fact that she wore no shoes. Her wet hair gave Jim the impression of cleanliness and though she was not the least bit unattractive, her crossed arms communicated a feeling of defiance. From different points of view, they both watched her son walk up the stone-lined path, dogs following, barking and wagging their tails.

A long time ago, as the story was told, when she was young like them, she got married and pregnant, though nobody really knew which came first. The baby was a boy and when he was three years old, his father dropped him, or so he claimed. Gilbert not only ended up with brain damage, but his eyes were crossed as well. Then dear old dad went out for a six-pack and never came home again. No husband and a developmentally disabled child caused the woman to become an outcast of sorts, and even her own parents would have nothing to do with her. Folks can make up reasons for not coming around. Jim knew about that, first hand. He called them lines—long invisible lines that nobody sees, but they're there just the same.

This woman was tougher than most gave her credit for. She managed, on her own, to get Gilbert enrolled in public school, and even though he was now twenty-two, he was going to graduate from high school on Friday. The state supported them, but in the shadows of the night, a male visitor might on occasion visit, supplementing their income; some things cross any lines.

"Mornin', Gil!" the bus driver offered in a heavy New England accent, but got no reply. Instead, the boy stopped and stared at Jim for just a moment. The boy-man meets the man-boy.

Gilbert took his seat in the front, right behind the driver, and pressed a notebook to his red plaid jacket. From where Jim was sitting he could see "GILBERT D." written on the upturned collar. To him it seemed a waste of time because everybody knew whose jacket it was. After all, Gil wore it every day. Jim let out a long heavy sigh, remembering that Gil's middle initial was "O," and when the kids were feeling especially hateful, they'd pick on GOD. More than once he had been in a full-blown fistfight in the back of the bus for defending Gilbert against "GOD IS A RETARD." Now he wondered if it would even bother him anymore.

Jim glanced back out the window of the bus, noticing that there was no car. Now he remembered: They never did have one. She hadn't ever had the opportunity to learn to drive. The bus driver pulled the doors closed, and kids began to chatter with one another, but Jim didn't pick up on it, as his eyes were locked on Gil's mom. He knew her—she was one of *them*, one of the faithful. Hidden somewhere under those folded arms was a cross, even though he doubted that she ever went to church. It was in her eyes, the strength. She didn't leave and she never quit. The voices were coming back to him again:

"Men don't walk out on their families, son," his father had said, "and they don't quit when things go against them either!"

"But..." he said to the car leaving in a cloud of dust, *"I'm not a man anymore. Look at me, Pappy, can't you see?"*

Jim held his head down in shame. As an adult, he had been bothered by memories of the past, and now as a child, he was bothered by memories of the future, but neither seemed "right" to him.

"Hi," she said, plopping down beside him, bringing his attention back to the inside of the school bus. "What ya doin' back here?" Though her accent made it sound more like "heah."

"Back here?" he wondered. "What did she mean by that?"

She was a pretty girl with long sandy brown hair and big smiling eyes.

"Groovy pants. Where are your beads?"

Jim remembered seeing them on the bedroom dresser. "I was actually supposed to wear those? How fashionating." Jim's experience in choosing clothes had, after all, been severely limited—he went from being dressed by his mother to being dressed by his wife.

He shrugged for a second before a smile came to his eyes. It was Eva, his best friend. They were an inseparable pair up until Mary entered the picture, but that was still two years away.

"How are you?" Jim asked and put a hand out on hers. They had lost touch after high school, and it was one of those regrets that he had carried around for a long time.

Her eyes went down to his hand and she made a funny face. "I'm okay. What's with you this morning?"

Jim let go. "What do you mean?"

"You're acting weirdo. Sitting in the middle of the bus and touching me. What? Do you want to kiss me or something?" She pulled the gum out of her mouth and waited.

Jim panicked. "What?"

"Oh, quit it!" she told him while putting the gum back in her mouth. Then she shoved him. "Scoot over." But it sounded like "ovah."

He moved over, feeling a bit uneasy.

"Well?"

"Well what?" he asked.

"Are you sick or something? Why didn't you call me?"

"I dunno. Was I suppose to?"

She shoved him again. "You went to the hospital. Remember? You were unconscious! You could have at least returned one of my phone calls. Your stupid little brother didn't tell you, did he? Where is he? I'll smack that wicked dense boy in the head."

Jim was laughing because Eva was always dressed like a nice little girl in her skirts and nylons and pretty shoes, but the truth was she could be as pissy as a drop of water on a hot skillet.

He shook his head no. "I'm sorry. They let me go on Saturday. Everything is fine."

Eva squinted her eyes for a bit longer, making Jim even less comfortable.

"Why are you looking at me like that?" he asked.

"I dunno. You seem…different."

This was one of the reasons that Jim was so fond of her—her uncanny perception.

"I'm having my period, okay?"

SLAP!

"Ow already! It was just a joke," he apologized with a laugh.

Eva gave Jim another shove, then pointed a short stubby finger with bright purple nail polish at him before turning around in the seat to face the front. She adjusted her books and her hair and picked at her nails just to make him stew for a bit. "You're too much of a baby to have a period."

Jim burst out laughing. "Says who?"

"Guys are wimps. Ask anyone."

"You mean ask any girl."

"I said anyone, not anything."

The two of them continued their banter all the way to school. When Jim took up with Mary it surprised a lot of people, because everyone had assumed that he and Eva would end up together. Well, everyone except Jane Benson, that is. As much as she tried with her match making, she could see that the two of them lacked timing. They were never in love with each other at the same time.

Keeping up with the class changes was Jim's biggest obstacle that morning. It had made him late to every class, but it was easier to find his seat that way.

He was sitting alone in the cafeteria, eating his lunch, when a girl he hadn't thought of in thirty years brushed past him with an unmistakable glare. Jim almost choked. He stood up and tried to catch her.

"Wait!"

But his actions didn't slow her down a single step. Two taller girls flanked her, the Wicked Mainah Witches, and they both turned to give him their famous "you-are-nothing-but-a-piece-of-scum" look.

"Damn, I hate the ninth grade," he said to himself.

Chapter Five

The girl's name was Mattie. She was his ex-girlfriend, and probably his first real experience with love, though he still wasn't sure. The talk around the school was that he had used her at a make-out party and dumped her afterwards. It was a story Jim had lived with until her memory faded, even though it was never the truth. He stood there watching her disappear, remembering that she would move away this summer, wondering to himself if he should take this one impossible chance to set things right.

Jim went back to the table and picked up what was left of his lunch and headed over to a garbage can, oblivious to the foot stuck out to trip him.

WHAM! His body hit the floor with unbelievable force. The room burst out in laughter, but the kid peeling himself up off the floor was not amused, not even just a little.

"You son of bitch! I'm gonna kick your ass into next month!" he screamed.

The kid who had tripped Jim was named Mark and was easily twice his size, but he backed up just the same. Somewhat crouched, arms pulled in and chin tucked, Jim looked out through black eyes, waiting like an animal. There was no question in anyone's mind what was about to happen, and the growing silence attested to it. Part of the bully wanted to just squash the skinny little bug boy, but another part of him told him to think better of it.

Jim calmed down and straightened up before turning and walking away. Fighting would solve nothing—

something that had taken him most of his adult life to learn. "Just walk away, Jim. Just walk away," he kept saying to himself.

Instead of trying to find Mattie, Jim went across the hardwood-floor hallway to the bathroom to wash his face. When the first bell rang, he found his way to the next class, took a seat in the back of the classroom and put his books under the chair. When he sat up, there was Mattie again, looking at him. Unblinking, he kept eye contact and then mouthed the word "please." She looked away and then turned back toward him again. Jim's heart started to race; he held up his hands to her as if he was praying.

Their exchanges didn't go unnoticed. A loud snort two rows away caused Jim to refocus his attention. It was the tripper from the lunchroom. Mark held up his hands, mimicking Jim. He pretended to say "please" and batted his eyelashes. Jim turned to face the front, his face growing red, now wishing he had finished the job when he had had the chance.

Mark started to hum a quiet little tune. Jim watched him. What was he singing? It was something familiar. Then all at once it hit him, filling his eyes with hatred. It was a dirty little song that the boys had made up to taunt him about Mattie. Some of the others turned around and started to snicker. They all knew the words. Then Mark raised his voice even louder, so that Mattie would hear. It was more than Jim could take. As if in slow motion, his entire body pivoted in the direction of the tune and his eyes zeroed in, consuming the bully.

This was about honor and nothing would stop him—not this time. The black-haired boy went berserk, launching himself at his tormentor the way a linebacker would go at a quarterback.

The kid, the desk and Jim all smashed against the wall at the same time. Other students scattered out of the way. Girls shrieked as Jimmy wrapped himself around Mark like a snake, burying his knuckles deep into the pressure points on his face. The boy was screaming from pain and surprise, but Jim held him with unchecked rage.

"You scream, you little girl! You scream loud enough so that they can all hear you. I know about screaming; let me teach you."

The rest of the classroom had broken out into a "Fight, Fight, Fight," chant.

Mrs. Gerret was only a first-year teacher, fresh from college, and didn't carry enough authority to stop it, but the wrestling coach, whose class had been interrupted by all of the yelling, did.

Jim kept yelling into Mark's ears, yelling to the point of hysterical laughter. His behavior was stupefying; no one had ever seen him so angry. There was a rumor going around the school that his brain got injured on Friday. Now they were wondering if it had made him crazy.

Coach Riggs took them out the back door of the classroom, dragging them down the hall by their wrists toward the gym. It was girls' PE, but they were all outside and the cavernous room was empty. Jim was certain that his arm was going to break. The coach was a big man, but if he didn't let up soon, Jim would fight him, too.

Old man Riggs swung his hairy arms forward, watching both of the boys go flying across the floor.

"You boys wanna fight? Then fight! Go ahead. Fight! Get it out of you! No one is gonna stop you, go on," he bellowed, making the room echo back.

Jim was more than happy to comply, but the big kid didn't want anything more to do with it and backed up, shaking his head no—parts of Mark's face were still numb.

Jimmy moved in. "You ever do that again and I will finish it. I'll finish you. Is that clear?" His tone carried the authority of the forty-year-old man.

Mark nodded yes, mumbling something about a joke.

"So is that it?" Riggs was yelling. "Are you through? Huh? Answer me!"

They both nodded, wincing at the sheer loudness of the man's voice.

"You!" He pointed at Mark. "Back to class."

The kid disappeared.

"You," he said, his voice now lowered but his arm pointed at him just the same. "Benson, isn't it?"

Jimmy looked back with defiance in his eyes, still disturbed.

"I don't like your attitude, son."

"I don't like your face, Riggs," Jim thought.

"Thirty laps, and you better be here when I get back."

Jim watched for a moment, then started to run. Thirty laps? He'd be lucky to do five. What choice did he have? The man went back to control his unattended class while Jimmy pounded the gymnasium floor with his feet.

Nearly an hour and a half later, Jim Benson stood outside the front entrance of the school, watching his bus drive away. He was late because he couldn't remember the combination to his locker. He let out a heavy breath and started down the stairs for a long walk on already sore legs, when he heard a car honking. It was Jenny.

"You wanna ride with us?" she asked, leaning out the window of a car Jim didn't recognize.

"Yeah, thanks," he said, crawling in the big back seat of the old tan Rambler.

"You remember Greg, right?"

Jim didn't but pretended that he did anyway. "Hey man, thanks for the lift."

"It's cool. We're headed to Para's for a slice first."

Jim nodded; Para's was the local pizza place.

"Heard you got in a fight," Jenny said, turning around and hanging an arm over the seat.

"Yeah, guess everybody heard by the way they're looking at me."

"What was the fight about?" Jenny's hands moved as she talked; they always moved as she talked.

Greg had adjusted his mirror to see better. Funny that Jim couldn't place him.

"Nuthin'." He wasn't about to tell. Besides, it was really between the Jim of the past and the Jim of the future. Mark was just a stand-in.

"You don't look so good," Jenny told him.

"That butthead Riggs made me run thirty laps. I thought I was gonna puke or somethin'."

Greg laughed. "He makes everybody run."

They all leaned as the car turned the corner at Long Sands beach and headed into York.

"Then he came back and bawled me out some more. But get this: He wants me to try out for wrestling next year!"

Jenny was watching him closer than he would have liked.

"What?" he asked, but she didn't answer. She just turned around and scooted closer to her boyfriend.

Greg and Jenny were playing footsie with each other outside of the pizza place after they finished eating. Jim was leaning against the car, looking down the street toward the beach; the food made him feel much better. The town was still deserted, and it would stay that way until summer vacation. Then it would be overflowing with tourists—which, incidentally, was considered to be one of the four seasons: Tourist, Foliage, Ski & Mud. He stretched his neck and turned it to the side, and poof! There she was again: Mattie.

"Hey," he managed to spit out, but she didn't reply.

Chapter Five

Jim pretended that he was trying to look around behind her. "What? No witches?"

No sooner had the words left his tongue than entered hag one and hag two. Jim rolled his eyes, but to his surprise, they walked right on past without even a "look." This made him suspicious because "when one doesn't get the 'look' and one knows that one should have, one should RUN."

"Hmmm," he thought, "what strange power the Queen has over these witches."

"What do you want?" The ice in her voice broke his thoughts.

"We need to talk about something. More than that, you need to hear something from me. Do you have a minute? I mean, is there someplace we can go?"

Mattie just stood there without answering, like a statue. It was humiliating, and he started to hope for a house to fall on his head and put him out of his misery, but she nodded and began to walk away. Like a gentleman, he said thank you to his sister and explained that he'd catch up with them after a bit.

"Don't touch me!" She whirled on him like a cat.

"Sorry. Look, no touchy," he told her, wiggling his fingers in the air. It was embarrassing just the same. He couldn't figure out what made him all of a sudden want to hold her hand as they walked.

"Where do you want to go?" she asked, but with the inflection in her voice Jim interpreted it more like: "I hope it is someplace where I can kick you in the balls!"

125

Jim shrugged; it didn't matter to him.

"There are some trails down by the river. Is that okay?" she hissed before flipping her hair.

"Yeah, that's fine," he gulped, thinking how he used to like it better when she smiled.   As they crossed the street and started down into the woods, she spoke up. "What was that all about in class today—the fight?"

Jim was surprised. She didn't know? How could she not know? Maybe it was a test, a witch test. "He had it coming, for a long time. You know that."

She stopped and turned around to look at him. "Know what?"

Oh, Christ, he thought, maybe she really didn't know.

"I thought you guys were friends."

Jim snorted. "Well we sure as hell ain't now, are we?"

Mattie didn't say anything, but her confused expression said it for her.

"So what do you want? Why are you here?"

Was she taller than he was? His mouth felt dry, and why was he so nervous? He put both of his hands on her shoulders for emphasis and though she tried to resist at first, she ended up letting them stay.

"Look, Mattie. I'm sorry. I made a mistake."

She threw his hands off of her multi-colored striped knit top and stepped back. "If this is about us getting back together, you're just a little late and you can just forget it!"

Chapter Five

Jim shook his head back and forth, trying to explain. "No, wait. No, that's not it. I mean I'm sorry about breaking up that way. I didn't know any better." He paused. "Don't you want to know why?"

She stopped and turned on him like a dog—a rabid dog with a foaming mouth and large teeth that say, "I'm going to chew body parts off of you."

He hated being around pissed women; they scared him.

"Why? What do you mean why?"

She was coming at him. She was going to hit him—he just knew it.

But she didn't. Instead she yelled, loudly, "You used me! That's why!" and then kicked him in the shins, hard.

"Son of a..." Jim groaned, almost falling down.

"You used me and lied to me and dumped me and the whole school knows about it! You made me cry in front of my mom!"

She tried to kick him again, but he dodged it. Jim's body was beginning to feel like it was in the first day of boot camp.

"I know you're mad; it's okay, but please don't kick me anymore. These are the only legs I've got, 'k?"

She halted her attack and Jim spoke up. "Look, didn't you ever even wonder why I didn't have another girlfriend?" He winced at his own use of the past tense. "*Don't* have another girlfriend," he thought.

Mattie's face twisted red and she was trying to kick him again. "Because you're an asshole! That's why!

And I told all of my friends what a creep you are." Her feet were swinging with wild determination.

Jim was almost out of breath from trying to stay out of striking distance and had to end up tackling her. They rolled around in the dirt and leaves, but Mattie was stronger than Jim and ended up pinning him on his back.

"Not the face, not the face," he whined, trying to cover himself up with his hands.

"You little baby," she cried before slapping at him.

Everything stopped and the girl just sat there on his stomach, looking at him. Sunlight filtered down through the canopy, caressing her shoulder-length auburn hair, bringing out all of the colors of the leaves now stuck to it. The river gurgled from some unseen location. Jim could feel her radiance.

"Ground cold?"

"Yeah...and sorta wet."

"Good. Stay there," she said, pulling her hair back to the side.

"I didn't break up with you because I don't like you, Mattie. I did it because I thought that I was falling in love with you, and I didn't understand it."

Mattie's face twisted into a whole new direction of pissed.

SLAP!

Chapter Five

"Are you stupid or what? That doesn't make any sense." SLAP! SLAP!

"Ow! Stop already with the hitting. I was scared, okay? I felt different about you. I didn't know what to do. It just got weird real fast."

Mattie put her face close to his. He was looking at her blue eyes and braces.

"I heard that you got hit in the head. I think that your brain isn't right!"

She had gotten too close and Jim was compelled to steal a kiss, which made her furious.

SLAP, SLAP, SLAP, SLAP...SLAP!

He didn't care; he was laughing at her from underneath his hands.

"What do you mean, you felt different?"

"I felt a certain way for you," he answered, but the tone in his voice and the laughter in his eyes were gone. He put down his hands and almost started to stammer the words, "You know."

Mattie was shaking her head back and forth. "No, Brain Damage Boy, I don't know."

Jim was exasperated and embarrassed. This wasn't going anything like he had hoped. He didn't think that he was going to have to explain every little detail to her. After all, she had been there, too.

"Somehow things just changed," he snapped his fingers, "like that. All of a sudden, I wanted to do other things with you, you know."

She didn't get it, so Jim raised his pelvis off of the ground a few inches, raising her up as well. She screamed and jumped up off of him, covering her mouth with both of her hands. Jim got up to brush himself off. Mattie just stood there, far enough away to feel safe from the sex maniac.

"So that's why you broke up, because you wanted to...do it?"

"No. Yes. No." He was going to lose this either way now. "It gets worse."

The tone of his voice softened Mattie's apprehension. She could tell that he was ashamed of something.

"Tell me," she said, wondering what could be so wrong.

Jim wouldn't look at her while he spoke. "Look...some of the guys must have noticed us at one of the parties. We must have seemed a little bit, well..."

Mattie was thinking, "They were make-out parties; that's what you were supposed to do: make out."

Jim was stalling.

"And so?" she asked, maneuvering so that she could see his face, but he turned from her, not wanting to let her in yet.

"So we were all talking one day, guy talk, sorta like conquest stories or somethin', I dunno." He picked up a rock near his foot and gave it a toss toward the river. "They wanted to know about us." His face wore a weak smile. "I musta been sorta conceited and like an idiot I told them."

"Told them what?"

"They wanted to know if I ever got a..." he turned toward her and dropped his hands making an overstated gesture toward the front of his pants. When she made the face of recognition, he continued, "if I ever got a...when I was with you. I said yeah, and that I kinda liked it." Jim exhaled. "But that wasn't the end of it, just the beginning. They must have been jealous or somethin', since none of them had girlfriends, and they made up that stupid song. I know you've heard it."

Jimmy watched her face; she seemed to be getting it now.

"Next thing I knew they started singing it every chance they got, and it made me mad. Any time you were around, they would hum it, and I just knew that you were going to find out. I knew your mom was going to find out. Hell, everyone was going to find out. Mattie and the Freak. So I broke up with you, right then and there in front of the Home Ec room. I didn't know what else to do. I didn't want to hurt you, but you got hurt anyway, probably worse. I'm sorry."

She didn't answer and he had no way of knowing what she was thinking. Jim wanted to keep on talking. He wanted to tell her something else, to say, "And then you moved away; we never said good-bye. You would never know, how I loved you so."

Mattie came toward him. "So that's what the fight was about? Me?"

Jim almost whispered it. "Yeah." He dropped his head, hoping that she could find a way to forgive him.

She put her arms around him and held him in the quiet of the woods. He could smell her and it made him want to cry, knowing that they were still on nothing but a dead-end trail.

Outside the cover of the canopy, the two of them stood watching Jenny and Greg from a distance. Mattie still held onto Jim's hand.

"I gotta go," she told him.

"Yeah, so do I," he responded, but neither of them moved.

She squeezed his hand very tightly and said, "Thank you," before kissing him on the cheek and walking away. Jim just stood there, hands in his pockets, wondering to himself if he had done the right thing. Wondering if forgiveness was really what it was cracked up to be.

Chapter Six

"Malibu," Greg raised his voice above the radio so that Jim could hear. "It looks like your old man."

Jim sat up and looked out the back window. It was their '66 that shot passed them alright, along with his father and Grandpa.

"Wonder where they're goin' in such a hurry?" He looked toward his sister for an answer but got none.

Greg's car pulled down the long gravel driveway to their house, an old white three-story home with black trim and steep roof lines, which was once the rectory for the church on the hill. Mrs. Benson was standing out front, almost as if she were expecting them all along.

"Hey, Ma," they both said in unison as the car drove out the circular driveway.

"Didn't I ever learn you two rotten children nuthin'? Don't call me 'Ma'!" she said with a hint of a smile while adjusting the bobby pins that held her hair "up"— the way she usually liked to wear it.

Jenny laughed. "Where were Pappy and Gramps going?"

Their mom's expression changed. Jim thought that she was going to cry. "Eddie. Eddie's come home." They were tears of relief.

Cousin Eddie came marching home again, straight from Vietnam. Three days ago he was up to his knees in Southeast Asian mud, and now he was sitting at the kitchen table with the adults. Jim knew how he must feel; three days ago he had been in hell, too.

"At least you won't have to go back to the ninth grade tomorrow, Eddie," he thought.

It was late and the kids had gone to bed, except Jim, who had hidden himself in the shadows on the stairs, watching. There was only one light on in the room. It was over the table, and enveloped with smoke from two cigarettes left to smolder in the ashtray. One was Mr. Benson's and the other had red lipstick on the end of it. Eddie wasn't wearing a shirt and his brown skin made the dog tags hanging around his neck stand out. Jim's father had his own set, and Jim remembered asking him what the small indentation on each tag was for.

"It's a tooth notch," he had told him. "When you're dead they put the tags in between your upper and lower teeth so they know who you were." Tagged like a dog, Jim thought. Death Tags.

While he talked, Eddie picked and scratched at the bug bites that covered his body. He was telling them about eating something called a "Rice Bird."

Chapter Six

"Yeah, so I'm out at one of the local bars, right? And they set down this food in front of me and I'm, you know, pretty drunk. So I ask them what the hell it is, and they tell me it's a Rice Bird. Well, it smelled pretty good and to tell you the truth it wasn't so bad, so I ordered another one and maybe even another one after that. Then, a couple days later I'm back at the LZ and I'm tellin' one of the other grunts about these birds and he just starts laughing at me. I say, 'What's so damn funny?' And he says, 'You dumb ass. It's called a Rice BUG!'"

The table roared in laughter. Eddie stuck a cigarette in his mouth and started rummaging around in the duffel bag lying next to his feet.

"Here," he said flipping something wrapped in clear plastic cellophane onto the table. "I brought one back."

The women screamed as Mr. Benson and Grandpa scooted in for closer inspection. It looked something like a giant cockroach. As they kidded around with the soldier, Jim couldn't notice how similar he and his cousin appeared, except that Eddie had deep blue eyes and was much more muscular.

"When do you report back, Edward?" Jim's mom asked while working on her needlepoint.

"One July. Until then, I'm free," he said with a wink.

"Well, President Nixon will be bringing everyone home soon enough," she continued.

Eddie shook his head as if he were disagreeing. "Auntie J, I don't know anything about politics. I'm not old enough to vote, just old enough to die." He had held his head very still as he spoke to convey his seriousness.

"That's right!" Jim thought. "This is 1971. Eighteen-year-olds couldn't vote. They were old enough to be drafted and go off to war, but they had no say in government—no say in the people in charge of sending them. This was a big deal."

"So, young man," asked Mr. Benson, "when are you discharged—done for good?"

"Maybe Two Six July, if my math is right."

Eddie poured himself another drink from the whiskey bottle in the center of the table and shot it down with a grin on his face.

"Damn, it's good to be back home. Brought something else with me, too." He reached back down into the bag again and set something else on the table.

Everyone stopped moving and watched as Eddie pulled his hand away from the object. It was a knife. Jim had read somewhere that combat vets could bring back anything that they wanted through something called an amnesty box, no questions asked. He guessed that it was the least the government could do for them. It seemed a little like going to the dentist; you get a prize if you don't scream too much. Jim began to wonder what else could be in that bag.

Grandpa reached out his old hand and picked up the K-Bar. It had once been his. He had carried the weapon in World War II, and he gave it to his son who carried the same blade in Korea. When Eddie was drafted, Jack Benson passed it on to him as a symbol of their strength, to keep him safe and to let him know that they were with him.

He set it back down and asked everyone to join hands before saying a prayer so muffled that Jim couldn't hear it. They continued talking, but Jim was tired and decided to sneak on up to bed. He had made it only a step or two when he heard his name called.

"Jimmy?" It was his father.

"Yes, sir?" he answered, dumbfounded.

"Goodnight, son."

"Goodnight, Pappy. Goodnight, everybody."

Opening his eyes, Jim thought for a moment that he was in some strange kind of dream, then the screaming that woke him up started again.

"Lai Dai! Lai Dai!"

There was running in the hall and Jim jumped up and threw open his door, only to find his father and Grandpa standing outside of Sarah's room, the room his mother had given to Eddie.

Someone had reached in and turned on the light. Eddie was crouched in the corner of the room with raging eyes and sweat covering his face, making his short black hair glimmer. Jim knew right away that his cousin was still asleep because his eyes didn't react at all to the light. Everyone else was squinting.

"Go back to bed now," Mr. Benson told them. "Go on. Everything is going to be all right."

Eddie seemed to come out of it with the sound of the old man's voice, though he was still breathing hard.

Jim nodded and went to his room. He understood bad dreams all too well.

The two older men took the soldier down the stairs, even though he was only wearing olive drab military issue boxer shorts and those dog tags. Jim was just closing his eyes when a light shot up from the floor of his bedroom. It was coming from an old heater vent that allowed the heat to flow upwards between the downstairs and upstairs floors. Voices followed the light.

Jim got out of bed and crawled across the floor to see what was going on. Just below the vent, he could see his cousin seated in the dining room.

His father lit a cigarette and passed it to the boy, waiting, knowing that there was something to get out into the open.

After what seemed an eternity to Jim, Eddie spoke.

"We..." He cleared his voice and sat up, then leaned forward and shook his head. "We were in stand down, hangin' loose, bored out of our freakin' minds. I just got off watch when I heard one of the Hueys was gonna go on an ash and trash run—you know, take one of the cherries for some boom boom. Me, I was hopin' for a doughnut dolly, just anything to get away from the ham and chokers. It was like a celebration for me anyway, cause I was so short I was playin' handball on the curb."

"Well, I grabbed some tiger piss and jumped aboard with a couple of the other blue-leggers."

Chapter Six

Eddie stopped talking and sucked on the butt of his cigarette, lost in thought, before crushing it out in a clear glass ashtray.

"I wasn't even wearin' a chicken plate," he said, shaking his head, "and not more than a few clicks out, POW! Peter Pilot is KIA from a watcher. Next thing I know we're on the ground in the shit number ten thousand."

To Jim it sounded like Eddie was speaking a different language; it was hard for him to understand what he meant.

"The gunner's goin' all-American, right, and the pilot is callin' for a dust-off so we grab our widow makers and look for cover. POW!" He made a sign with his thumb and forefinger. "The cherry gets popped. Man, we grab and drag but it ain't no good cause we ain't no DOC. Then it gets quiet, too quiet. I can see the bird from where I'm at, and the gunner and the smoke pouring out, whirling around. The cherry is dying but I don't even want to know anymore. 'I'm too short for this,' I'm tellin' myself, and those bastards will just send another one that looks just like him. But I look anyway and I hold him in my arms. I don't even know his damn name. He looks at me with those eyes and I watched him die. I felt him turn cold, somethin' I've done too much of. There's a part of you in the back of your mind saying, 'This could be me. Maybe I'm next.'"

Eddie just sat there looking like a tired little boy, then his voice went monotone as he spoke again.

"There ain't no heroes there. We ain't no heroes, not like you. We know that, and it makes it worse. We are just kids playing army. None of it is real, except for the dead—it's real to them."

Mr. Benson turned his head away, like he was ashamed or responsible or something. Jim could tell that by the way he held his body. Eddie closed his eyes, his chest rising and falling; he bent his head down, looking at his fingers.

"So I got up to scout the area, look for the shooter, and I found him laying in the brush with a great big hole in his guts. He was dead, too. We traded the cherry and they traded him—just more numbers for somethin' that wasn't even a battle."

Tears started coming from the corners of Eddie's eyes, "Then somethin' moved in the bushes and I scream 'AMF!' and laid down fire. The other blue-legger came running and he laid down fire. After it was over, we waited, then I went in."

His voice was cracking, making him hard to hear. "It was a kid. A twelve-year-old kid with a rifle that probably didn't even work and I killed his ass. I didn't know. I swear to Christ I didn't. I wouldn't have shot. Damn the bastards for sending their children to do their killing."

Grandpa's eyes didn't blink.

"Man, that was three days ago. When I got back to base camp, they handed me a ticket to the world. 'FIGMO!' I said."

Chapter Six

He looked at the men for the first time. "Nobody tells you how beautiful it is over there, except the parts that are all blown to hell. I'd wake up sometimes out in the bush, soaking wet and covered in bugs, wondering why I was there. What did I do to deserve to get sent to a hell like this? Man, I wanted to play baseball. You know, I get back to the States and they're all waiting for us outside the gate. You saw them. They weren't welcoming me home. They weren't saying, 'Hey, good job.' Oh, hell, no. They were spittin' at us and screamin' at us, waving those homemade signs. 'Warmonger! Murderer! Baby Killer!' And they were looking at me, the G.I. Joe in the back seat, and they're right, man. I am a baby killer."

Mr. Benson put a hand over his eyes.

"They don't want us here. They don't want us there. What did I do wrong, huh? No one asked me if I wanted to go. It wasn't a choice; I was just another D-I-E. I didn't want to go; they made me. That's where they made me go."

Eddie's body was shaking and his face was covered with sweat and tears. "How am I going to tell my dad? How am I gonna tell my mom or my little sister how many people they made me kill? Huh? Somebody tell me." But the men didn't have an answer for him. "Why did we go there? Why?"

Jim pulled back away from the vent. He had seen enough. Part of him knew why, part of him had always known why.

"You went for me, Eddie," Jim wanted to say, "and you don't even know it, 'cause nobody knows it, or if they do, they won't tell you. In some twisted way, you went for me and all the guys like me. You can't see it now, but I never had to go—because of you and your sacrifice, I was never forced to go. You went, and so did Pappy and his dad and his dad before him, but I didn't. I didn't *have* to go and my kids don't *have* to go. You stopped it; it was you who broke the cycle. It was your pain, Eddie that changed this nation more than anyone else's, because you gave us a kind of freedom that none before you were able to win. You taught us the value of a soldier's life. I wish there was a way that I could explain it to you so that you would understand just what a hero you really are."

"Mom? What's Eddie's bag doing out here on the porch?" Jim asked while he was going out the door the next morning to catch the bus.

"I don't know. He was sitting on the bench there not too long ago. I know that he has been up for a while. He said that he isn't used to sleeping for more than a few hours at a time, and he really appreciates the quiet of the mornings now. He probably just went for a walk to the beach."

"It is so foggy, though. I hope he can see the trail. Oh, well, I'm gonna go."

"You're awfully early."

"It's okay. I'll see you later, Ma."

Chapter Six

"Boy, I'm gonna beat the breath out of you if you don't quit callin' me 'Ma'!"

Jim laughed and let the screen door slam behind him. A horn sounded in the distance, from the Nubble Lighthouse. The sound brought with it a sense of warning. Jim's eyes followed the rock wall that paralleled the driveway, while the dampness in the air forced him deeper inside his jean jacket. As he turned the corner, he started cursing to himself, having forgotten to get the combination to his school locker. Jim was thinking that he would have time to run back when they jumped him.

WHAM! He saw flashes of blue but before Jim could react, they hit him again and again. The taste of salt and copper filled his mouth. Someone had a hold of his arms and wrenched them behind his back. As Jim's eyes focused he could see Mark, the kid he had attacked at school yesterday. Jimmy couldn't believe that he had been so stupid. He knew that there was no way to win a fight, because even if you did, they'd usually come back for revenge. This was a payback for a foolish mistake and Mark had come with his two older brothers to settle up.

"You see me? You see this?" Mark was shaking a baseball bat. "Huh? Who do you think you are, skinny boy?"

Jim didn't say a word and just stared as Mark prepared to take a swing. When he stepped into range, Jim swung up his right leg as hard as he possibly could, connecting his black Converse tennis shoe to the underside of the batter's open jaw. The boy and the bat tumbled backwards while Jim let out a laugh, just before his face was driven into the gravel.

WHAM! The blue came back again. The brothers were kicking him to death.

The three shots fired into the air from the .45 were deafening. Everyone froze. Jimmy rolled to his side, coughing, and could see the outline of someone standing off in the fog.

Edward Benson had been sitting on the porch earlier that morning, enjoying the air that was no longer polluted with explosions, when he heard a vehicle pull up somewhere in the mist. Eddie had moved silently from the porch through the wet meadow to assess the situation with gun in hand. If this had been a few days earlier, in a different land, the intruders would all be dead. Instead, he chose to withdraw, put on his uniform and wait.

"Dung Lai Caca Dau, Du Mi Ami!" he screamed in Vietnamese.

A large wet spot appeared in the front of the biggest brother's pants; Eddie was dressed in his jungle fatigues, his arms and face in camo paint. He was walking slowly toward them with both hands on the gun, leveled at their faces.

"This is what we call a number ten thousand, you little pricks. Berry bad!" He spoke with an Asian accent, moving the weapon from face to face. Mark still rolled around in the gravel, holding his blood-smeared mouth.

"Don't kill them, Eddie," Jim pleaded, watching his own blood drip from his face to the gravel. "For Christ's sake, don't kill them." He tried to pick himself up but couldn't find the strength. "I started it...I started it, okay? Just don't shoot them."

Eddie acted like he didn't hear his younger cousin's pleas and continued to advance until the muzzle of the weapon was pushed into one of the brothers' eyes, making the boy cry.

"Why shouldn't I, Jimmy? Huh? Here it is, no more problems, the final solution." He pulled back the hammer. Nobody dared breathe. "I know. Let's all go, but you first, asshole," he told the kid.

Jimmy thought that the boy's eyes were going to burst from his head.

"It's what you want, right?" Eddie continued, his voice sounding more distant. "Nothing more to worry about...you're goin' to die anyway...why not now?"

"Because it's wrong. Don't do it, Ed." Jimmy said while closing his eyes, waiting for the inevitable, seeing so much of himself in his cousin.

The hammer eased back with a click. "Lucky for you my cousin is the answer man." Eddie screamed, "POW!" and that boy's pants also turned wet. Eddie backed away, circling them, still swinging the weapon from face to face.

Jimmy could see the fatigues clearly now. They were covered in dried blood. "God," he thought to himself, "those are the clothes he was wearing when they got shot down. Eddie's flipped. He's out of his freakin' mind."

Cousin Edward stopped when he noticed the baseball bat lying at the edge of the driveway. He had been a pretty good baseball player in high school and even got a scholarship to go play for a community college in Minnesota, but his number was drawn before he had the chance to go.

"What do we have here, boys? Huh?" he reached down and picked it up. "I used to practice my batting with a rock pile, but my bat never looked this bad." He came closer to the oldest kid, and even though Eddie was only a year or so older in age, he was decades older in experience. "What do you use this for?" he asked, pushing the end of the bat into his face. "Huh?"

The big kid started blubbering so much that he couldn't answer, but it was clear enough to Jim: mailboxes.

"SHUT UP!" Eddie's voice was angry. "Here's the way this is going down. You pukes get your pussy asses in that car and forget that this ever happened. Anything comes of it and nothing will stop me from finding you. NOTHING! You remember this: I was here the whole time and you didn't see me, you didn't hear me. You won't see me coming the next time either. THIS IS OVER! GET IT?" He pressed his face against the kid's. "That your car?" he whispered. The kid followed the point of the bat toward the Fairlane, outlined in the fog.

He nodded. "My dad's."

"Oh." Eddie grinned. "Sin Loy."

Chapter Six

The gun exploded again, shattering the side and back windows.

"Looks like it needs some glass," he said, backing away from them. "Go! And take this piece-of-shit coward with you!" he told them, kicking gravel at Mark who was still on the ground.

"Don't forget what I told you."

Jim had managed to make it to his knees. Eddie pulled him up and they both stood there watching the car wheel out of the driveway and disappear.

"Thanks, Cuz. They would have killed me."

Eddie didn't respond right away. He was picking up the last of the shell casings. "Don't sweat it. I gotta go," he said finally, and vanished as mysteriously as he had appeared.

Jim staggered down the driveway back towards the house, almost running into Jenny and Daniel.

"What happened?" Jenny's voice was almost frantic when she saw his face.

Jim wondered why she hadn't heard the gunshots, and if she hadn't heard, maybe nobody else had either. "I was running back to get something and fell into that rock wall," he lied—but she would believe it in an instant because her little brother was the biggest klutz on the planet.

"Come on. Let's get you back and cleaned up."

Embedded in his cheeks and forehead were tiny pieces of rock and dirt. Jim winced as his mother scrubbed them out of his face.

"Oh, hold still."

"I'm tryin', Ma, but it kinda hurts."

"You're staying home today. I think you are too tired."

Jim didn't argue with her. He couldn't care less if he ever went back to that school.

"Dad, would you mind driving the kids to school?" Mrs. Benson asked. "I don't know where Eddie is."

Grandpa nodded and pointed toward the door, but his eyes never left Jim, making him a little uncomfortable.

"Bye, Jimmy. I hope you feel better," his little brother said.

"Thanks, Danny. I'll be fine," he responded, but the truth was that his ribs hurt so bad that he thought they might be broken.

"No, Ma, you are not going to put that junk on me."

"It's iodine. You need it to stop infection."

"No," he protested, "you are not going to turn my face orange. The only thing I need is an aspirin, okay?"

There was a tone of authority in his voice to which she was unaccustomed.

"Fine. When your face gets infected and you end up scarred for the rest of your life, don't blame me. I do what I can with you rotten kids."

"Oh for cryin' out loud, Ma. Would you quit it already? Huh? It's a little scratch. I'll be just fine."

She shook her head and went to get him his aspirin.

Two hours later Jim woke up on the couch. He rolled over and groaned, holding onto his sides. The smell of

Old Spice after-shave filled the air. Grandpa was seated in a chair across the room, watching him. Jim lay there a moment longer, trying to wake up, wondering to himself why his grandfather always dressed so well. Jim couldn't ever remember him wearing anything other than a white shirt and dark slacks. Not like his father, who usually wore a tee shirt and jeans—unless, of course, he was in his uniform or going to church. Grandpa's thin gray hair was slicked backed all the way around his head and the black-framed glasses made his eyes look bigger than they really were.

"You okay, young fella?"

Jim sat up. "Yeah, I'll be okay. Just a little stiff."

The old man got up and came toward him, sitting down on the coffee table. He reached out and took a hold of one of his grandson's hands, turning it palm side up, and vigorously started to rub it. Jimmy felt the tension inside of him begin to dissipate. The longer his grandpa massaged, the more relaxed Jim felt, and the boy thought he might fall back to sleep.

Grandpa began to hum a gospel song while he rubbed first one and then the other hand.

Jim loved the sound of his voice, and later, in his adult life, his grandfather would call just to leave a message on his recorder. The message would say, "You're looking good, young fella, with muscles popping out all over your body. You're doing good. Just keep going," or something to that effect. For days, Jim would keep the message and play it back again and again, always thinking the same thing: "Everyone needs somebody like Grandpa."

"Say there, Jim. You know when I was a young man, I used to run a lot, too. Did I ever tell you that?" he asked while looking into his grandson's eyes.

"Well, I did. And you know something? Sometimes I'd fall, just like you did today." He grinned, making his old eyes crinkle. "Oh, I fell a bunch. But you know what the one thing that I always remembered to do was?" He stopped rubbing and waited for an answer.

Jim tried to think, sorry that he had stopped, and just shrugged.

"I always tried to catch myself with my hands," he said, holding both of his hands out to demonstrate, still watching the boy's face. "I didn't notice a mark on your hands, Jim, can you explain that to me?"

Jim didn't know if the old man was speaking figuratively or literally. Part of him knew that, either way, it would produce the same answer. It made him think for a moment that maybe he hadn't tried to catch himself after the accident. That he had just let himself fall. The thought bothered him some, because it meant that he would have to share in the blame.

The old man slapped Jim's leg and got up and walked away, leaving the boy-man to sit and further contemplate his circumstances.

Chapter Seven

He walked out the back door after lunch and headed toward a faded trail through a field that was alive with wild flowers. The fog had lifted, revealing an almost perfect early June day. Jim stopped and knelt down to look at something on the ground. It turned out to be nothing more than a rock, but it had sparkled like gold. It made him think of his wife, because she had always been his sparkle even though he was no longer her rock.

This was her field. It had always been hers, and his mind carried him back to the first time they met. She had been sitting right over there with a large black and orange butterfly perched on her head. There was a flower behind one of her ears, holding back long white-blond hair. Mary's eyes had sparkled in the sun, like emeralds.

At first Jim had planned to just keep walking right on by her, thinking that she was probably one of those flower children his father had warned him about.

"I know you," she said. "Remember?"

It was the sound of her voice that had stopped him from taking another step; it had such an incredibly beautiful tone. Jim turned and looked at her for the first time. She nearly took his breath away.

"What did you say?"

"You live over there, in the white house with that dome thing, right? Your name is Jim Benson."

Jimmy nodded back. He was trying to place her, but with no success. She had to be wrong because he would never have forgotten meeting someone like her, not ever.

She had smiled, letting him off the hook.

"Oh, I guess you don't remember me. We only met once, and that was a few years ago. I live in that house across the street now. My name is Mary."

Jim wanted to cry all of a sudden and stomped his way through the tall grass toward an opening in the rock wall on the hill. He wanted no more memories, but then the lyrics of a song filled his thoughts.

"Well then, what's to be the reason for becoming man and wife? Is it Love that brings you here, or Love that gives you life?"

The words were from "The Wedding Song," his wedding song—and they had also followed him back through time to bother him. His future had become his past and his past the future, though neither of them seemed any more real to him than the other.

As if she were still there, he could hear her words again.

"Wow," she had said, looking at the lightning bugs they caught later that same summer.

Jim shook the bottle a bit. "Fire in a bottle," he had told her, liking how close their two heads had gotten.

She must have felt the same thing, because right after that, Mary had kissed him right on the cheek.

Jim put his hands to his ears, trying to make his memories leave; the longing was too much for him to bear. He picked up the pace, and was now running through the field, not considering the path that his feet had chosen. Through the passage in the wall and up the gravel driveway, Jim stood face to face with what he had been running away from the whole time.

The native stone and wood church was a remarkable work of art. Built in 1897, it was complete with a porch, a bell tower and the ever-present lightning rods that adorned most of the taller buildings throughout this part of New England. Black lines running down the sides of the grounding cable bore witness to the fact that the church had weathered its own share of violent encounters with the sky.

"YOU!" he screamed at the building. "Why don't you leave me alone?"

Jim glared at the church, his anger giving rise to fury, and pounded his way up the hill. "Elohim, or whatever You call Yourself, answer me! Why are You doing this to me? My name is not Job! This isn't the way it is supposed to be. None of these things ever happened to me! You are changing it. You want me to fail. How can I have a perfect life if I don't know what is going to happen? How can I get my life back now? You've ruined it, just like You ruined my other life. I didn't ask You to interfere with my life. Leave me alone!"

His face was red, with little bits of blood and spit flying from his mouth as he spoke. "WHAT HAVE I DONE THAT WOULD MAKE YOU DO THIS TO ME? I'LL TELL YOU WHAT! NOTHING! I DID NOTHING TO DESERVE ANY OF THIS!" he screamed as he made his way up to the top of the stairs and stood before the door.

An unexpected calmness overtook him, and he felt himself swaying. It was Mary talking to him again.

"Have you ever been inside?"

"Yeah. I even know where the key is. They showed me and said that I could come in anytime at all. I just have to be sure and lock up."

"You're teasing me."

Jim jumped up on the bench and reached on top of a beam, pushing aside a small rock, then held the key out for her to see. "Believe me now?"

Mary eyed the key like it was some kind of forbidden treasure. "Open it up," she said, biting her lower lip, eyes filled with excitement.

Moments later the click of the old latch was followed by an even older creak as he slowly pushed open the big arched wooden door.

"Do you think anybody is in there?" she asked, trying to peer inside.

"Just God. He's always here. Can't you feel it?"

Chapter Seven

Mary eyed him suspiciously, questioning his sincerity.

"Oh, they are so beautiful," she told him, referring to the stained glass windows, as she made her way through the doorway.

Jim's mind raced from his memory of the past to a memory in the future, a time just after the accident, when he was drunk and in a fight with Mary.

"You come back here!" he slurred. "Don't you walk away from me! Look at me. You can't accept me anymore, can you? You can't accept the way that I am now. You can't accept this!" He tore off his eye patch and threw it at her. "Or this!" Jim bellowed while waving his mutilated hand in the air. "Or this either." He undid his leg and hurled it, but it went astray and ended up crashing through a stained glass window that Mary had spent months making.

He could still see her bending down over its remnants. "I...I didn't mean that, Mare...I...I," he had told her, but the damage was done.

"The glass darkly," she said while looking at him. "Why?"

Jim's mind brought him back to 1971 again, where he found himself with his head leaning against the church door, key in hand.

"I am so tired of all of this. I can't carry this burden much longer," he said aloud, unlocking the door and walking in, but the little girl Mary was with him again.

"It smells so good in here, like old wood," she said, making exaggerated sniffing sounds.

It had been quiet for a while and Jim remembered being somewhat mesmerized by her presence. The girl had a way of making him feel that way.

"This," she paused, "this is where I want to get married." And she turned to look at Jim.

He had watched her for a moment before saying, "Okay," and that had been when he knew for sure that she would one day become his wife.

He discovered himself standing halfway down the main aisle, staring at the colored light that filtered through the meticulously crafted windows. Then something moved at the front of the church. There was something behind the red velvet curtain.

"Who's there?"

A rather tall man with dark curly hair and brown eyes stepped out into full view; it appeared to be a priest.

"Oh, I'm sorry, Father. I didn't mean to intrude."

"It is quite all right. Please, feel comfortable."

The man had a strange accent that Jim couldn't quite place and as he walked forward, the light from the windows bounced off of the stranger, illuminating his head. The impression it gave sent shudders through the boy-man.

"My name is Michael, and I believe that your name is James. Is that correct?"

Jimmy nodded back suspiciously. "You meant Father Michael, right?"

"No, just Michael," he replied without elaborating.

Michael came a few steps closer before sitting down on the red-carpeted stairs that led to the altar. He clasped his hands between his legs.

"How do you know my name?" Jim stood defiantly, folding his arms across his chest, demanding an answer. The disturbing thought that sprung into his mind was that maybe this stranger was somebody God had sent as a stand-in, somebody willing to take up the fight that Jim presented.

Michael wasn't answering the question and the silence began to make Jim more than a little uncomfortable.

"Well, then," he continued, his apprehension changing to anger, "since I'm here and all, would you mind helping me with a few problems I seem to be having about…faith?"

"Of course. I have come to help you, James."

"Help me?" Jim was confused; the way he had said it led him to believe that the priest meant something else. "Help me with what?"

"Finding your way."

"My way? What the hell are you talking about? I'm not lost."

"You're not?"

"No."

"Then what are you doing here?"

"Look," Jim started, but he was at a loss for words. He didn't have an answer to the question. "I was just looking for something to do. That's all."

Michael started to nod as if he understood, but stopped halfway through it.

"So you came to a church?"

"Forget it. I'm outta here. There ain't nuthin' here I want anyway." He started to turn to walk away when his mouth got the better of him.

"You know what really pisses me off about you and all of this religion crap? You are nothing but a bunch of hypocrites and liars, and you play on man's biggest fear: dying. Why can't you just leave people alone? Huh? God doesn't exist and you should be ashamed of yourself for what you do. People would have a lot better life if they knew that this was all there is."

"Is that what you think now?"

"You heard me say it, didn't you?"

"I don't believe you meant it. I think you are just suffering."

"Suffering?" Jimmy mimicked him.

"Yes. Suffering is nothing more than your inability to understand."

"I understand plenty, pal. Back off."

"Why are you so angry?"

"I've got my reasons and they are none of your business."

"On the contrary, God is my business. Why do you speak to me as though you were the one who was chosen to sit in judgment over man? What concern of yours is another man's soul? You can scarcely manage your own." Michael rose and so did his voice. "James, the path has already been blazed, so that even one like you should be able to follow, but still you are lost. Where will you find your salvation?"

"Salvation? Who asked you, anyway? Huh? Don't preach to me! Look behind you, fool," he said, pointing to the figure of Jesus nailed to the cross. "Your God killed Him, too. Do you really expect me to believe in *that*?" He cupped his hands over his mouth and yelled, "It's cruciFICTION!" Michael's eyes turned black and he lowered his head ever so slightly. "Hear what has been written: *'There is salvation in no one else, for there is no other name under heaven that has been given among men, by which we must be saved.'* Without Jesus there is no forgiveness for man's sins and no hope of eternal life; there is no forgiveness for *your* sins. Jesus said, *'And whoever welcomes me does not welcome me but the one who sent me. I and the Father are one.'*"

"Don't you talk in riddles to me, priest!" Jim yelled. "You are more foolish than the rest because you believe in three Gods instead of one!"

"Can't you even understand that there are three parts to your existence? That you *are* the image? Why do you miss the simplest things about your life? Is it so difficult for you to believe that the one who gives your body life, who gives life to all things, could be more than what you yourself already are? Can you not understand the words, *'Let us make man in our image?'*"

Jim knew that he was referring to the book of Genesis but couldn't figure out a way to contradict him.

"Why, James, is it easier for you to stray down the unmarked path than to follow the one that you know in your heart to be true? Tell me: What wealth have you exchanged for your denouncement?"

"What?" Jim was shocked at the question posed to him. His face grew even redder in anger. "Are you implying that I have made some kind of agreement? Is that what you are saying—that I have been given something in return?"

The thought slammed into Jim's brain. He had been given a chance to start over in some upside down world.

"What is it, James, that could make your feet run so rapidly toward evil?"

"NO!" Rage now consumed Jim Benson. "I DID NOT TRADE!" he bellowed with everything that he had. "I never abandoned God! HE ABANDONED ME! DO YOU HEAR ME? HE ABANDONED ME!" Tears began to well up in the boy's eyes. "He doesn't want me anymore. He threw me away like a piece of garbage. All I ever wanted in my life was to be wanted—just to be wanted. I DID NOTHING WRONG! How dare you try to overwhelm me!" Jim wavered back and forth, letting out feelings that he had refused ever to think of. "The absence of God in my heart does not mean the presence of evil. Don't you know that?"

Michael waited for the boy to calm down. "Tell me, child, what could be so horrible? Is it worse than He has suffered?" he asked, pointing to the large crucifix. "Has your soul known more suffering than His? He *is* the Son of God. They are *one* God and He suffers with you now." The priest spread out his arms. "You know why Jesus came to earth, and you know why He died, as proof of His love for you, for all of mankind. A king born as a man, with more love and power than the world has ever known since its creation. A man who suffered like you, because He was like you yet without sin. Lift up your heart to the Lord, James. He is the way."

"No! You don't listen! I did not trade, you hypocrite! You and your talk of trades. Isn't it you and your GOD who promised rewards in the afterlife? Isn't that just a trade? Suffer now and be rewarded? What about *this* life? What about now? Do not accuse me. I have made no deals. Do you hear me? No deals. Who do you think you are?"

"Who do you think I am?

Their eyes locked, neither willing to yield.

"I have nothing more to say to you, because in my eyes, you are all the same. You with your beads and your crosses and your 'follow mes.' You teach lies and that makes you a liar. You tell people to believe, and believe they do, but where is God when they need Him? You offer nothing to help the living, only a promise of salvation or a threat of damnation. Well, I'm here to tell you: I know damnation. God did everything to me and I believed. I was His friend. You don't know what He did to me."

Michael looked as if lightning bolts were going to come from his eyes. "Then forgive him."

Jim was astonished. "Forgive God?"

"Yes, if that is where you place the blame, lift your burden with forgiveness."

"What in the...NO. I won't. You're nuts. Whoever heard of forgiving God?"

"Then in your tomb you will stay, boy."

"Because I won't forgive God?"

"Because you won't forgive yourself."

"Have you ever listened to yourself, priest? Make up your mind already."

"You act like this is a game, James. It is not. This is about the way you live your life."

"Yeah? Well I'd rather walk around the way I am than grovel on my knees the way you do. And you know what else?" he continued, pointing at the priest. "I can't think of a single damn thing God has ever done for me except give me this miserable existence He calls life."

Then, as if it had appeared out of thin air, Michael held up a neatly folded piece of paper. "Remember this?"

"Where'd you get that?" Jimmy watched him in disbelief.

"You left it in the offering box. It is how I knew your name."

"Give it back."

"Why? Are you ashamed of it now?"

"It's not yours! Give it back!"

Michael unfolded it and began to read it aloud: "Flowered fields and butterflies, she whispers dreams in moonlit skies. I pray for truth and not for lies, for I see my life within her eyes. The gifts you give I plainly see, the gift of love you gave to me; I thank you God on bended knee."

"Shut up," he mouthed, while no sound followed.

"And this? Do you want this back as well?" Michael asked, holding up a silver crucifix that may have come from a Spanish ship. It was the treasure that Jim had been searching for the day he almost drowned. Somehow he had found the courage to go back for it, and had put it in the offering box, along with the note.

"No."

Michael was coming toward Jimmy now, and though the boy wanted to move, he couldn't.

"Very well then. Now think, child. What is it that God wants from you right now? What have you missed? There is still time. Think. Let me help you."

"NO!" Jim barked back.

"You cannot hide. You will face this. You must decide. Let me help you to put your anger aside and open your heart."

"Stay away from me," Jim screamed, more like a frightened girl than the angry young man he thought he was. As he turned and headed for the door he heard the man speak.

"This isn't over, James. Your journey has just begun."

The door slammed shut, but Jim could still somehow hear Michael's words floating through the air as he raced down the hill.

"Oh, God, I thank Thee for the gift of life and the promise of a new day. Help me to meet the world courageously as one who puts his trust in Thee and trusting is unafraid. Make me strong to temptation, brave in danger, hopeful in defeat, confident of Thy guidance. May I live in quietness and peace."

"You stupid priest. How in the…" Jim was halfway down the driveway when all of the pieces fell into place. Jim hadn't written that letter yet. He didn't even know Mary, so it was impossible for the priest to have it. Trying to skid, he fell into the gravel, sliding to a dusty stop. He made it to his feet and ran back up the hill to the church door only to find that it was locked.

"Let me in," he yelled while pounding. "I know you're in there. Come out and face me. Who are you?" Despite all of his theatrics, the door remained closed. Jim gave up and started walking toward the field, talking to himself. "Can't you just leave me alone? I just want to be left alone. I don't need your help. Go away."

Exhaustion and the morning's adventures caught up with him, causing him stop. He bent over, holding onto his sides; the pain in his ribs was almost unbearable. Sweat dripped from his forehead, making the maze of cuts on his face sting. At this moment Jim felt worse than he ever had in his entire life. If he hadn't known better, he would have been certain that he was dying.

Chapter Seven

The boy dropped to his knees, still breathing hard, and tilted his head back to look at the blue sky above him. Someone had once told him that no matter what it looked like, no matter how many clouds might block the view; the sky was always blue. Jim could see no clouds anywhere; it was almost as if they didn't exist.

"Son of a…" he groaned. "What is happening to me? Where am I? Who am I?" He was trying to catch his breath.

"I didn't make a trade. I didn't. I just wanted things to be back the way they were. That's all. I wanted to be a husband that my wife could be proud of, a father that my kids could look up to again. What was so wrong with wanting that?" Jim said to the sky. "You made me into a freak. How could I stay with them the way that I was, huh?"

He laid his head down in the tall grasses and flowers and closed his eyes. "I wanted to grow old, not be old all in one day. Don't You understand? Don't You understand anything?" He drifted off into a dreamless sleep.

"Whatcha doin' out here?"

Jim opened his eyes to find little Sarah staring at him with those concerned blue eyes of hers.

"Hi, little girl. I guess I just fell asleep," he said and started to rub at his face, but stopped because it hurt.

"You've got stuff stuck in your cuts," she told him with a sour expression.

"Yeah, I know. I'll get it cleaned up at home."

"Did you fall down again?"

"Yeah."

"'Cause you were running?"

"Yep."

"Maybe you should go slower."

"Maybe."

"Hmm, hmmm." She hummed a little tune.

As he lay there watching this little yellow-haired girl sing, he wondered what had happened to her. She had always been his little sister, his shadow, but in their adult lives he rarely saw her at all. What happened to her to make her change? Then it dawned upon him. Maybe nothing happened to her; maybe he just quit being her big brother.

Jim managed a smile at her. "How come you keep singing that song?"

"It's a secret," she whispered. "I get to sing at graduation."

"You do?"

"Yeah," she replied, still whispering. "Wanna hear my part?"

"Sure."

"Then you'll have to wait until Friday," she giggled. "I told you it's a secret."

"You better sing to me or else," he threatened playfully, reaching out with a hand to tickle her.

"Noooo. Stop it. Get up and give me a ride."

"Oh, all right. Help me up."

Sarah took his hand and pulled with groaning sounds until her brother was on his feet.

Chapter Seven

"Now don't kick at my ribs 'cause they're still sore." He put the little girl on his shoulders and headed for the trail that led to the house.

"I love you, Jimmy," she whispered into his ear.

"I love you too, sweetie."

"I'm gonna go, Ma. I'll see you this afternoon," Jim hollered as he went out the front door the next morning to catch the bus. He couldn't walk very fast, despite the coffee and aspirin; today he found it more difficult to walk than when he didn't have a leg. The thought of having to go back to classes again made his stomach churn. Part of him wondered why he should even bother, because the school was going to burn down this summer anyway. Jim couldn't move. The school was going to burn down. How come he hadn't remembered that before? How could he not remember something like that? The school had lost everything, including everyone's "permanent records."

"Jesus," he said out loud. "I can stop it."

"Bye, honey!" he heard as he stepped off the porch.

Outside in the driveway, leaning against the Malibu, was Eddie, smoking a cigarette.

"Jimsan," he said, looking over the top of his sunglasses, "let's go for a ride." His presence postponed Jim's concerns. Eddie made him nervous.

"How come you have Pappy's car?"

"The Chief wanted me to drive him into the working place this morning—thought that I'd rather have this today instead of Aunt Janey's wagon." He gave his cousin an exaggerated shrug. "He really just wanted to talk, you know?"

"Yep."

Eddie held open the passenger-side door of the shiny automobile. "Come on. I'll give you a ride to the escuela."

"Sure," he answered, but the apprehension inside of him was growing. Jim was sure that his cousin also "just wanted to talk."

The sixty-six lumbered up to the bus stop just as the bus pulled away in a cloud of blue smoke. Eddie sat there, listening to the rumble with one hand on the wheel and his body slumped against the door. His eyes seemed to be frozen to Jim as he stared out into oblivion. It struck him as odd, because normally his cousin was constantly looking around.

"What ya doin' here, Jim?"

"Huh?"

There was an uncomfortable silence for a moment, and Eddie seemed to be maintaining it on purpose.

Jim couldn't help but notice that Eddie was wearing his jungle combat boots. There was something written on them. "What's that 'Bt' for?"

"What?" Eddie turned to look at him.

"On your boots. You wrote 'Bt.' What's that?"

"It ain't wrote; it's burned on. That's B positive, my blood type, so the DOC can patch me up."

Jim didn't want to ask any more questions.

"Well, well," Eddie said while lighting another cigarette. "Want one?" He held the pack out.

Chapter Seven

"No. Thanks, though."

Eddie pulled off his G.I. Joe hat and hung it on the rearview mirror, then messed with his hair for a second. It occurred to Jim that with the white tee shirt, his cousin looked just like a soldier who was home on leave.

Ed turned his head, looking up the road in the direction that the bus had gone. "We could go up there," he said, motioning with his cigarette, "to that town. I know of a bakery and a cutie who works there. Mercy! I told her she had nice buns," he grinned, blowing out smoke.

Jim was shaking his head because he knew that underneath those dark aviation sunglasses were the two wildest eyes on the planet. "Maybe," he thought to himself, "if I got out and ran like hell I could still catch the bus."

"Or," Ed continued, now motioning the other direction, "maybe that way, toward that Nipple lighthouse." He sucked on the Marlboro while contemplating the choices.

"There's always a fork in the road, isn't there, Jim-me?" He didn't look back—just kept on talking right out the window. "You come to places like this all of the time."

Jim was still feeling uneasy and now he had to pee. The coffee that he had with his breakfast had gone right through him.

"That's it, isn't it? One way you know you should go and the other way you think you want to go. It's always the same problem—trouble all around all of us all of the time. Do what you want to do, or do what you should do? Either way, you'll always wonder if you did the right thing. My daddy always told us that the man who wants to do what he should do is the luckiest man alive."

He seemed to be thinking of something for a moment before continuing. "You know what, Cuz? There were a lot of nights I'd lay awake over there, out in the bush, wondering if I would ever get to come home and drive a car again, or even hold a girl's hand." His voice sounded dark to Jim.

"You have lots of strange things like that in your head when you think you're gonna die—stuff people take for granted. I mean, you never think about holding a girl's hand until you see your buddy get both of his damn arms blown off. It made me afraid. I mean, my life would be over if something like that ever happened. Even though I told myself that I could get through it, I know I wouldn't. I'd end up just like them, with that same look on my face. God, I didn't want to end up that way. I'd rather just die, you know?"

Jim didn't answer. He didn't want to talk about this because he *did* know. "Cuz," he thought, "it ain't like that, at least the being afraid part. What really scares you is that you find out that the people who loved you all of a sudden don't anymore, making you dead. What's worse is that nobody told you you were dead— you have to find it out yourself. That's when it starts on the inside, the pain they'll never see. The kind that eats at you, into you, until you go insane, because there is nothing that you can do to stop it. You keep hearing the voices. The ones that say things like 'Where's my leg? Where's my leg?' and you tell them that it's gone and to go away but they keep searching for it, begging for it, until you wake up screaming."

"I once thought that the reason I was there," Eddie said, "was because I had to learn something. I don't know why I have to always look for a reason. I mean Grandpa had a reason for going. Hell, he's like the defender who took on the world, and won. We all tried to be like him, but we didn't have any reason to fight, so I guess I tried to keep on making up things to get me through it.

"I dunno what you're gonna do, Jimmy. I just know you're gonna have to decide one way or the other. You can stay here or go; both are hard. Maybe you'll get lucky and the war will really be over with and you won't have to decide nuthin', but I don't think so."

"Eddie, thanks for being there yesterday. They probably would have killed me if you hadn't come along."

Ed just nodded back real slow, still looking away.

"Still, a part of me feels sort of sad for them."

"SAD?" Eddie's voice rose to a scream. "Looky here. I got sent halfway around the world to go die in some jungle that, in thirty years, nobody is gonna give a flip about for less than went on here yesterday! I sure as hell ain't gonna come back home and put up with any crap in my own damn yard! SAD? For what? Their miserable existences? Oh, I know—their mistake of wanting to show up and bash your head in! Or is it their wasted lives that make you wanna cry? Yeah, I get it. Let's be sad for them because if they got a second chance they wouldn't do it again, is that it? What is wrong with your brain, son? Huh, Jimmy boy? Here's your wake up call, pal. You can't fix them. They have to fix themselves—get it? What the hell do you think your father would do if he knew there were three sons of bitches with baseball bats waiting for his boy at the end of his driveway? He works in a prison, for Christ's sake!"

It was true. Jack Benson had accepted a promotion to get off the surface ships, so he could be at home with his family more often and keep from being relocated. Jim remembered going to work with his father once, and only once. He had never wanted to set foot in that place again. What always stuck with him was the memory of a little piece of paper stuck on the wall with yellow tape. It read:

"With only a little sense you will walk on the main road. The only fear will be straying from it. It is easy to stay on the main road, but people just seem to love being led astray."

That was it in a nutshell: a whole building full of people who had gone astray.

Jack Benson changed from working there; he grew more compassionate, which was strange because many of the other guys who worked there were just the opposite. Whenever possible, he did an extra special job, because he understood that his cooking was one of the few things that those soldiers had to look forward to. He told Jim that he tried not to think of their crimes, or whether or not their punishment was just—he would just try to see the man on the other side of the line. The day of the visit, he told Jim something just before they went onto the base.

"Some of these men that you are going to see have done terrible things to others, and in turn have done terrible things to themselves. The difference between these men and others is that you can see their bondage. These are men who are held hostage by their past and by their unwillingness to change their future. If you learn anything from this, son, it should be this: You shall reap what you sow."

His father had a party at the house once, and it seemed like half of the town showed up. Jim overheard a conversation about the prison; it always came up. One of the guys was saying that anyone who committed a violent crime should be executed—an eye for an eye. Another fellow argued no, because it went against the Ten Commandments, and in God's eyes there is no difference; killing is killing. Somebody else said that it was better to just lock them away in solitary confinement for the whole sentence. Then they wanted to know what the Chief thought—after all, he worked there.

"All of you seem to have the same idea: that penalty is prevention. I disagree with you," he told them in his slow, matter-of-fact manner. "You want to increase the penalties to prevent the crime; in other words, you want to use fear to control. Penalty is nothing more than persecution, and each one of you would differ in the method.

"I will never be able to know why some of the guilty do what they do, and I believe that some of them don't either. Some are crazy and some just have no fear—not of you, or of the law, or of God. But none of that matters, because most folks are focusing on how to correct them *after* they have committed their crimes, rather than before.

"I think our biggest mistake is that we *expect* them to do what isn't right and then lie in wait for them like predators. It seems—to me, anyway—that in this way we become just like them.

"What should concern us the most is our own attitudes. I mean all of us are locked within our own ideas, just as they are locked within those walls. The bondage that I see is not of chains. They too, see it, and for them I am afraid.

"Reach out to them before they stray. Accept them as your equal before they sin. Show them your light. I am not their judge. I merely feed them. I feed the sheep."

"Listen, Jim. That thinkin' ain't right! You just pack that 'sad' away. You hear me?" Eddie was furious and Jim was sorry that he had brought it up.

"You're right, man. Thank you." He knew that his cousin was pretty messed up and conceded.

The concession caught the soldier a little off balance and he shut up. Jim put a hand to the door handle. He had to go pee. Then the very worst possible thing happened. The radio, which had been barely audible, got turned up as loud as it would go.

Jimmy's face turned white. "This isn't good," he thought. "This isn't good at all." It was Credence Clearwater Revival and they had just started banging out the draft-induced enlistees' national anthem, "Fortunate Son." He knew, just by the way that Eddie's body was starting to move, that he was going to piss his pants.

"LOCK AND LOAD!" The driver yelled, his head bouncing to the beat of the drums.

Eddie grabbed the gearshift and slammed it into first while smashing down on the accelerator pedal. Three hundred and twenty-seven cubic inches of Chevrolet engine came roaring to life. Gravel flew from the spinning tires and Jim was sure that it had to be hitting the ocean some five hundred yards behind them. The car sat motionless for a moment, then lurched forward onto the blacktop. Smoke rolled off of the tires, rubber departed and the car screamed to life. The Malibu slid sideways across the painted line and began to fishtail its way down the road, throwing Jim hard against the car door.

Eddie's voice couldn't be heard over the engine, but he sang anyway.

"Some folks are born, made to wear the flag, ooh, they're red, white and blue, ooh."

He caught second gear and Jim's neck almost broke as he continued.

"And when the band plays 'Hail to the Chief,' Ooh, they point the cannon at you, Lord."

Ed shifted to third.

"It ain't me, it ain't me, I ain't no senator's son, son."

He looked at Jimmy, whose face was well on its way to turning green.

"It ain't me, it ain't me, I ain't no fortunate one, No!"

Eddie was back in Vietnam, riding around in some chopper and Jim was in some hellish Disneyland, trying to find something to hang on to. Jim noticed the speedometer; the needle read sixty, and they were still accelerating.

"Shift!" he screamed, not wanting the transmission to explode through the floorboards.

The car squealed around the narrow, winding road toward a small rise just ahead. Jim braced himself as the '66 hit the crest and left the pavement.

Eddie let out a Midwestern war whoop. "WAAAAAAAHOOOOOO!"

Jim's idea of a high school dream machine landed nose first, causing him to leave the passenger seat and smash his head on the roof of the car. Eddie accelerated even faster.

"Some folks inherit star-spangled eyes, Ooh, they send you down to war, Lord, and when you ask them,

'How much should we give?' Ooh, they only answer 'More! More! More!' Yow."

The blue rocket was nearing eighty-five miles an hour and Jim knew that if they didn't slow down before the next corner, they'd both be tomorrow's headlines.

"It ain't me, it ain't me, I ain't no military son, son. It ain't me, it ain't me, I ain't no fortunate one, one."

They passed a county sheriff going the other direction. Eddie let off of the gas and started braking. He reached up and turned down the radio while watching his rearview mirror. Jim noticed that the hat was still hanging on.

"Think he saw us?" Eddie asked with a big grin.

Jim stared back, thinking, "No, we were invisible, ya moron."

The cop had stood on his brakes, leaving a trail of blue smoke. Jim could see his red lights snap on just before they disappeared around the turn. Eddie pulled the Malibu over at a wide spot, then shut the car down. He looked over the top of his glasses at his cousin, grinned some, and then flicked the butt of his cigarette out the window.

The patrol car slid in behind them and Jim could tell by the way the cop had gotten out his car that he was some kind of mad. The deputy slammed the door shut and cussed his way toward them. Eddie just sat there, looking straight ahead like he was the smartest kid in class, his glasses now resting on the dash.

"Get the hell outta that car, boy!"

Jim just knew that he was going to piss his pants now. He grabbed onto the vital part and squeezed it for insurance.

"Isn't this Jack Benson's ve-hic-call?" he barked into Eddie's face. Eddie stood straight and tall, much like a good soldier in boot camp.

"Sir, yes, sir."

The cop gave him a good face-to-face look, but something was already different about the officer. His voice was a little—not much, but a little—calmer.

"You got some i-den-ta-fa-cation on you, boy? Like maybe a license from NA-SAW?"

Eddie reached for his wallet and Jim reached for the door handle. The cop started to say something to Jimmy, but nothing was going to stop him now. He was already in zip and flip mode. The big-bellied man could see what Jim was doing and turned toward Eddie again.

"You like scaring the piss out of little kids?" he barked again, but Jim detected a bit of sarcasm.

"Sir, no, sir."

The man looked over the military I.D. then gave Eddie another long, close look. Eddie stood at attention, not moving a muscle. The only sound was Jim's pee hitting the dirt.

"How long you been back, son?" he asked much quieter.

"Five days, sir!"

The cop looked down at the ground, then back to his cruiser and took in a long breath. His voice was civil as he spoke.

"You probably have more reason to want to do what you just did than I'd ever know about. Hell, I'd probably do the same thing. But you listen to me, son." He paused, pointing to Eddie with the I.D. card. "You made it home in one piece, so don't go out and celebrate by killing yourself, or anyone else for that matter."

The deputy turned his attention to Jim who was getting back inside of the car and shutting the door; Jimmy knew it but avoided eye contact.

"I don't ever want to see you doing this again. You understand what I'm saying here, soldier?"

"Sir, yes, sir. Thank you, sir."

The deputy handed him back his I.D. and told him to be on his way. Before Eddie got back in, he heard the man say, "You did okay over there. I just wanted you to know that."

His cousin nodded and looked at the lawman for the first time. Jim had no way of knowing it, but this would be the only time that Eddie would ever hear someone say that to him. Ed closed his door, put on his shades and lit another cigarette. Jim watched him, wondering if he was thinking about the pat on the back that he had just been given.

"Later, Ed. I appreciate the lift." Jim was lying when he said it, but he doubted Eddie cared because he left the parking lot with a nice long burner.

He hobbled up the stairs to the school and as he passed the principal's office, someone called his name.

There was something about the school he needed to tell the office about, something important, but couldn't recall it.

"Mr. Benson?"

The boy stopped and backed up a few steps, just enough to see inside the doorway.

"Did you call me?"

"Jimmy, come in here, please," the woman said, though with the Mainah accent it sounded more like "heah."

Jim turned and came towards the woman behind the counter with funny-looking hair and glasses. "For crying out loud," he thought to himself, "what are you wearing?"

The lady had on lime green eye shadow, matching lipstick, a green silk scarf tied around a beehive hairdo, green culottes and, to complete the ensemble, green gum that she smacked while she talked.

"You were absent from school yesterday. Do you have a note?"

"Note? Ah, no, I ah, must have forgotten it. Sorry. I'll bring one tomorrow."

"It is the last week of school and some of the students take the opportunity to play hooky," she said, staring at him with no expression, "maybe at the Fun-O-Rama?" She tipped her head down, looking over the top of her black pointy-rimmed glasses. "Now, you're not going to tell me that you are one of *those* kind of boys, are you?"

Chapter Seven

Jim pulled his long black hair out of his eyes while the lady reached a hand over to a big rotary-dial telephone.

"Tell me your phone number and we can get this cleared up right now."

"My phone number?" Jim didn't have a clue. "Look at my face! I had an accident yesterday, okay? I wasn't playing hooky. I'll bring you a note tomorrow." He was still trying to think of the number when a loud voice barked right behind him.

"BENSON!" the man said, while putting a hand to Jim's shoulder. "Just the young man I was looking for." It was Happy Jack, the principal.

Jim turned to see the man's huge smile, hence the nickname.

"How is your head?"

Then, like a big green parrot, the lady piped in, "Oh, that's right! How *is* your head?" Pop! She popped a tiny chewing gum bubble.

"I'm okay. They let me go home on Saturday. Just ran a bunch of tests, but I'm fine."

"Good. Glad to hear that, but let's you and I go sit down where we can discuss your conduct in Miss Gerret's class on Monday."

Jim looked briefly back at the funny-haired lady. She had the look of satisfaction and the "I'm-glad-I'm-not-you" look all rolled into one.

The door closed, and for the next twenty minutes or so, Jim was treated to a lecture on all of the evils of fighting. Luckily, when he was released, the hair lady was on the phone, and he was able to sneak away.

Back in the hallway, Jim was standing in front of his locker when the strangest thing happened. He knew the combination. Other things jumped into the front of his mind as well, like the names of the kids with lockers around his. It was quite a feat for a kid who couldn't even find the right hallway two days ago.

"Mr. Benson?"

He turned to find his English teacher standing just outside of her doorway.

"Are you going to join us today?"

"Yes, ma'am. I was in the office."

She gave him a perceptible nod but didn't move aside as he walked by into the classroom. Jim took a seat across the aisle from Eva, next to the open slide-up windows that ran the length of the large classroom. Behind the teacher's desk, in the front of the classroom, were black slate chalkboards.

"Hi," he said with a smile to her while sitting down, but Eva looked right through him, until she noticed the cuts on his face.

"Kinda messed up, huh?"

Eva whipped her head back toward the front. The teacher was still standing out in the hall, giving the Stalin treatment to somebody else.

"Wow. What's up with that?" Jim asked her.

The girl whipped her head back again, this time pulling her long hair to the side and holding on to it. "What did you say?"

Jim thought about the problem for a moment. "You know what's wrong?"

Eva just stared at him. "Oh, God," he thought, "she's giving me the look!" He dropped his eyes away from hers to avoid being burned by the lasers and found himself staring at her legs. She was wearing the shortest black mini-skirt that he had ever seen. Unconsciously Eva pulled at the clothing, but it didn't help.

"I heard you and Mattie got back together." She said it like it was rehearsed. The teacher had come back into the room and started to write something on the blackboard, causing Eva to whisper the word "together."

"Together!?" Jim panicked. "Back together? Is that what happened? How did that happen? Everything happens without me. I just apologized for something that happened a long time ago." He clenched his teeth together and looked out of the window. This was all happening way too fast and out of his control.

He turned and leaned over into the aisle, careful to make sure that the teacher was still busy writing. "Why are you so mad at me?"

Eva's face blushed; now she was really mad. Jim couldn't figure girls out anyway, but she was always a puzzle. He watched her start to write something on a piece of paper in big loopy letters.

A fresh summer breeze blew in through the open window; Jimmy took a deep breath. The teacher started to talk but he wasn't listening. He began to drift off in thought again, asking himself just how any of this could be happening to him. A note landed in his lap.

Unfolding it, he read:

YOU ASKED ME TO GO THE GRADUATION DANCE ON FRIDAY NIGHT!! ARE WE STILL GOING?! OR ARE YOU TAKING YOUR NEW GIRLFRIEND!!!!!!!!?

"Crap!" he muttered. "Look at all of those exclamation points. How do I get myself into these kinds of messes?"

"I know," he told himself. "I'll just tell them both that I'm married to an old woman with two kids. They'll understand."

"Mr. Benson?"

Jim looked up. The English teacher was standing right in front of him with her hand out.

"You have something that you would like me to read to the class. May I have it, please?"

He was sure that in her spare time she was a prison guard. The entire class had turned around to watch the show, most of them grinning. Mattie was up in the front corner, snickering. Jim put the note in his left hand and dropped it out the window, not breaking eye contact with his teacher.

"Oops."

The class burst out laughing, but the woman was not amused.

"Quite humorous, Mr. Benson," she said, grinning an evil smile.

He was dead, no doubt about it.

"Well, now," she continued while peering out the second-story window at all of the other trash below. "You may either spend the rest of this period outside, picking up the litter, or you can have a return trip to the principal's office."

Jim glanced over at Eva, who seemed rather pleased with herself. This was all her fault.

"Can I use that trash can?" he asked, pointing at the one beside her desk.

"Yes, just bring it back empty."

There was open sneering and chortling as Jim made his way to the front of the room to pick up the little brown can. Suddenly a booming voice echoed throughout the classroom.

"THE BENSON BAT CAVE IS OPEN."

The whole class burst into laughter again, even the teacher. Jim didn't get it at first, so as a bonus he turned toward everybody with a confused expression. Then it hit him: His zipper was down. Embarrassed, he fumbled for it but ended up dropping the can and spilling trash all over the floor. The room was in an uproar. Jim noticed that the teacher had had to turn around to conceal her laughter. Humiliated, he scooped up the trash and left the room.

"I hate the ninth grade," he mused. "Where is Eddie when I need him? "

Chapter Eight

Everyone had heard about the famous Jim Benson. In just a couple of days, he had become the most talked about kid in school—just none of it was good talk.

He was thankful that lunch was over and that he was now in the safety of Mr. Samuel's classroom, a civics class. There was a certain amount of maturity in the class, because most of the students were seniors trying to fill the credit requirements to graduate.

Mr. Sam, as the students called him, was a man of fifty who was all too aware of America's problems; it was, after all, his job. Violence throughout the country had grown to epic proportions for a civilized nation. The recent assassinations of John Kennedy, Robert Kennedy and Martin Luther King, Jr. were, to Mr. Sam, like losing stars from the sky. To him, those men had been compass needles for a generation needing direction.

The issue of the moment was race, and the decisions that the leaders were making in 1971 were leading toward forced bussing and integration of schools.

While sitting on the edge of his desk with a loosened red tie, Mr. Sam asked, "Do you think that one day everyone will be the same color?"

A lot of the students were nodding yes.

"Oh, I'm not saying in ten years or even in one hundred years from now. I just wonder if you think that it is possible. What do you think?"

His manner of teaching brought genuine interest in the classrooms; he was casual but very calculated and tried not to involve the usage of the twenty-year-old textbooks.

"Yes. I think so," said a girl in the back of the class.

Others in the room chimed in, agreeing.

The discussion wasn't going in the direction Mr. Sam had hoped for. He was looking for opposition. "How about you, Ben? You're from a Navy family, aren't you? If I remember right, you told me that you have moved around quite a bit. What do you think?"

"NO. Never will that happen. Not ever." His voice projected a little louder than he would have liked.

Everyone turned around to look at the defiant one, especially Jim. He knew firsthand what it meant to be a military brat and how different they were because of all of the moving around. They never had "real" friends, not like what the local kids knew; instead, they had acquaintances. When you stay in one place, you have the opportunity to resolve your differences with others, even if it takes a long time. But when you have to move on, the problems are always left hanging, like dirty laundry on a clothesline. In a way, the acquaintances left behind become frozen in time; they never change and the kids that move on never know what becomes of them.

"Well. Tell us what's on your mind, Ben. Why not?" Mr. Sam eagerly asked.

Ben was clicking a black ballpoint pen imprinted with the words "US Government," which could be defined in any dictionary as "go ahead and steal this and anything else that you want labeled with this inscription."

The kid wouldn't look up as he spoke. Jim thought that maybe he was embarrassed because of his acne.

"I doubt that any of you have any friends other than white ones, or, for that matter, even really know somebody who isn't white. I've had to change schools six times, and I know what prejudice is. I know what it is like to be the only white kid in the classroom. I can tell you what it is to be hated just because of the way you look. Sometimes it might be the other kids, or their parents or even the teachers, but it's still the same. You are hated on sight."

Mr. Sam nodded, hoping the boy would continue, but it appeared that he wasn't going to. The veteran teacher encouraged the reluctant student. "Help us with this. Do you remember anything in particular?"

"Yeah. Once, on Valentine's Day, when I was in grade school, all of us had paper bags lined up along the windows of the classroom with our names on them. They were our mailboxes and I had spent the night before filling out all of my little cards, and making sure that I didn't forget anybody."

Ben kind of laughed, but it was a somber laugh. He was still staring down at the desk, though the clicking had ceased.

"Man, I couldn't wait to get to my mailbox. I guess I was kind of hoping that this girl I liked might give me a special one or something. I was just young enough not to be able to figure it out, though, you know?"

It was so still in the classroom that Jim could hear the boy draw in a long breath.

"But when I got to finally get up and go get my bag, it was almost empty. I didn't even get one from the teacher."

No one spoke. The students' eyes began to drift away from Ben to other, less uncomfortable points in the room.

"We had all dumped them out on our desks, so everyone knew."

The memory was painful for the senior. It was apparent on his face.

"I've lived other places," another kid with short brown hair and freckles added, "but it's not like that here."

Ben turned and looked at the kid with the freckles. "It's like that *everywhere*. Here it is quieter, that's all. People act like racists, even most of you. I hear you talk about the war and you call them 'slopes' or 'gooks' or something. You talk about Negroes and call them 'niggers,' like it makes you feel good. It's easy to do stuff like that and it doesn't matter what color you are, either. I've heard it all.

"My mom tells me that people are different, and that is okay. It's when you try to make them alike that you start to have problems. She's right, too; nobody wants to *be* the same as anybody else—just treated the same."

"Mr. Samuel," Ben concluded, sitting up a little and clearing his throat, "I don't think people will ever be the same color. They hate each other too much."

"Yeah, but once you know somebody that all changes," the kid with the freckles piped in again.

"Maybe," Ben answered, "but that takes time. It doesn't matter anyway. Color isn't equality and it won't change the hatred we have for one another. Color is just convenient. That's all."

"Thank you, Mr. Reeze," Mr. Sam said, watching the young man. "I appreciate your thoughts." He looked around the room and then toward the door, checking to see if anyone might be listening.

"Anyone here still read the Bible?" Mr. Sam's use of the word "still" was intentional. Eight years ago the government had taken away one of his favorite teaching tools, religion, and forbade him to ever bring it up in a public school again. Already, he could see all too well the effects of this regulation on the student body. This was devastating to a man who had almost become a minister, but whose uncanny rapport with young adults ultimately led him to this profession instead.

Most of the kids nodded and a few even grinned. This wasn't the first time Mr. Samuel had asked the question, and the unwritten rule was that what went on in their discussions was kept quiet. This man was the student body's favorite teacher, their mentor, and more often than not his after-school hours were spent counseling confused teenagers. The students knew where to go when they were in trouble. They confided in him and he upheld their trust.

"Do you think that you can find any answers in it?"

Jim sat open-mouthed, still finding such rubbish offensive. He looked around the room for support, but nobody else seemed concerned, and it suddenly made Jim feel like the witch from the Wizard of Oz. "I'm melting, you evil, evil Bible thumper. I'm melting." Then those thoughts were interrupted by a memory. Just before his accident, Harrison, Jim's friend from work in Manson, had spoken up in favor of school prayer at a school board meeting they both attended.

"You know," he told them from the podium in his deep voice, "I suppose that it doesn't seem like any big deal to stop a little prayer before a football game, but I see a bigger picture being painted here. Just last month I was summoned as a defense witness into court. Yep, I raised my right hand and repeated after the court official, saying, "I swear to tell the truth, the whole truth and nothing but the truth, before the court." He waited and watched his audience for a moment. "I didn't say 'so help me God.' This makes me believe that God has not only been expelled from our school

systems but has also been escorted out of the courtrooms as well. When did this happen? Now I don't know about some of you, but as for me, I've always believed in my heart that the judicial system was based upon honesty and God." Harry gripped both sides of the podium while keeping his eyes on the folks seated in the folding cafeteria chairs. *"This raised some questions with me, like can there be truth without God? And can there be justice without truth? I think not, and if it is our governing body that makes these decisions on the premise of individual freedom, shall one who hates justice rule?*

"What is next? Will our money one day say, 'In this we trust?' I am afraid for a nation that was built with God but now is on the road to abandoning Him. A road built by us well-meaning folks who, in trying to keep from stepping on our neighbors' toes, are in effect teaching our children to look away from prayer, to look away from God. Is this the message that we really want to communicate?"

Jim sank down into his seat, remembering how much he had admired and respected what Harry had said.

"President Abraham Lincoln once said," Mr. Sam continued, "'Read this book for what on reason you can accept and take the rest on faith, and you will live and die a better man.'" He paused, letting them contemplate the words. "Ben, my point here is that anything is possible with God—anything. Don't give up, son. I know you've had a hard road, but your eyes see better than most. At times everything can look bleak, but with faith in the Lord, you'll see the bad times through."

Ben Reeze nodded back. A stone had been laid between his uncertainties, a stone of understanding.

During the ride home, Jim shared a seat with Gilbert, and in his misery he compared himself to the man-boy who stared out the window. Somehow he didn't feel that he belonged in this world any more than his companion. They both existed someplace else, but at the same time, were with each other here and now. It made him feel like he was a strange visitor from another planet, now marooned on the Planet Freak. Gilbert's head whipped toward Jim's brown eyes just as the thought entered his head. Jim was on the verge of screaming again—his imagination was getting the best of him. Gil's eyes looked off in two different directions while he grinned his yellow smile. As soon as he got off the bus, Jim was going to have a beer. That's all there was to this. If he was going to go crazy, he was going to go drunk.

The brakes squeaked to a halt at Gil's house and Jimmy moved aside enough so that he could get out. Gil's mom was waiting again, the dogs were barking again and she seemed to be looking at him again.

"Git off the bus, Jim." Gil said, standing.

Jimmy squinted at the smell of the foul breath. "What? This isn't my stop."

"You know what I mean," he told him as he brushed past.

Jim watched him leave and noticed Mrs. DeDana. Hope hadn't dropped her eyes from him, but this time Jim just turned his head away. He didn't want to play anymore. As the bus lumbered on its way, Jim noticed a piece of paper folded in half on the floor. Gil must have dropped it. It was a graded English paper assignment entitled "Themes." The teacher had written in red ink pen "Name?" and awarded the grade "D–." Scrawled along the bottom was written, "Gilbert, your connections are weak. You didn't follow directions about a central theme! See me." He slipped it in between the pages of one of his own books.

Across the aisle was Eva. She hadn't spoken a word to him since the note incident. Maybe he was invisible Jim again.

"Hey," he called, trying to break the ice. "I like the pink better."

Eva turned her head toward him. "What?"

"The nail polish. I like the pink that you are wearing better."

She didn't reply but he knew she'd at least talk to him now. Mary taught him how to do that. "Women," she whispered once, "always love a compliment. It tells them that you care enough to notice the little things."

"Scoot over," he told her with a push to make himself a little room.

"Well, if it isn't the two-timer himself," she replied smugly.

"Oh, quit it already, will ya? I don't know how this got all mixed up. I just apologized to her for the way that I treated her. I was wrong, okay? I had to tell her; it was the right thing to do. I guess she's thinking something else now—I'm not sure."

"You never apologized?" she sounded shocked.

"No," he replied, with a rush of guilt.

"Never?"

He shook his head again, feeling his face begin to redden. "Look, this doesn't affect us, does it? I mean, of course we are still going to go. You're my best friend. Why wouldn't we?"

The bus squeaked to another stop and more kids bumped past him on their way out. Eva was smiling at him, liking the way he always referred to her as his best friend.

Jim reached a hand out onto her long hair and swirled some of it around his finger.

"Does she really think that we are going out together again or something? What did you hear?"

"Boys are so dumb. They don't know anything. All's I know is that she thinks that you guys are going to go to the dance. She didn't have a date and now she says she does, or is really, really hoping for one."

Jim let go of her hair, looking away, but she could read him the way that best friends always do.

"You can't very well call her up and say, 'Forget it.' That would be just like doing what you did before." She paused, knowing that this was one of those awkward subjects that they had never broached. Her stop was just ahead and she readied her things.

"Why don't the three of us just go together as a group?" she asked without looking at him. "It's not like we are married or something. It might be fun." She put on a smile but it was a sad smile just the same.

All of her life Eva would be that way, putting others ahead of herself. She was an easy person to love. Jim wished he had kept up better relations with her as the years passed by. Good friends are so rare to find, yet somehow we abandon them along our way.

"I'll call you a little later tonight, okay?"

She nodded back and stood as the bus stopped. Jim grabbed onto her free hand and gave it a squeeze.

"Thanks," he whispered into her ear as she passed.

Through the window he could see the sunlight illuminating her long sandy hair. Then she was gone. Jim's head bobbed backward as the bus started off again. Depression was setting in. It seemed to him that no matter how hard he tried to do the right thing, he always just ended up making somebody he loved feel like dirt.

He got off the bus alone when his stop rolled around and just stood there, listening to the motor whine and the gears change until the sound was replaced by the chatter of chipmunks and blue jays squawking.

"Hi, honey. How was your day at school?" His mother's voice startled him. She was walking his way, carrying something all wrapped up in tin foil.

"School was okay. What's that?" he asked, gesturing with his free hand.

"Your grandmother and I made fresh pies today. I thought that Wilma would like one. Would you please take it over to her for me?" she asked, holding it out for him.

Jim exchanged his books for the pie. "Wilma?" He wasn't exactly sure just who Wilma was.

His mom gave him an exasperated look. "The blind lady, across the street in the green house." She watched him and was about to say something else when he spoke up.

"Oh, yeah. Sorry. I'll be right back." He still didn't have a clue who his mother was talking about but figured that he could find a green house across the street.

"No, I want you to stay and visit with her now. She likes the company. You two can sit and have some pie. Now go on, she's waiting!"

Ordinarily Jim would have turned and walked right across Shore Road without looking, but something made him stop. He looked to his right and then to his left and when he did, he couldn't help but notice the mailboxes again. It must have been hers that didn't get destroyed.

"W. O. Seyte. That's weird. Why would a blind person need a mailbox? Oh, maybe she's Asian? It's a Braille Box!" Jim laughed, thinking he was funny, and headed across the road.

After walking down a short dirt driveway he stood outside of the yard, listening. Louis Armstrong was singing "What a Wonderful World." The voice filled the air and danced through the leaves of the giant maple trees, causing Jim to slow his steps.

"I see trees of green, red roses, too. I see them bloom for me and you. And I think to myself, what a wonderful world."

It was a magnificent old house, he thought, sitting on a stonework foundation with green cedar-shake siding and a big screened-in porch.

"I see skies of blue and clouds of white. The bright blessed day, the dark sacred night. And I think to myself, what a wonderful world".

The yard was overgrown, and even the trees hung down to touch the ground. Jim was certain that he had never been here before, but at the same time it was sort of familiar.

"The colors of the rainbow, so pretty in the sky, are also on the face of the people goin' by. I see friends shakin' hands, sayin' 'How do you do!' They're really sayin' 'I love you.'"

Maybe Danny mowed her lawn sometimes, or it could be that he had seen it from the trail behind her house. Lord knows he had walked by here enough times, hadn't he?

"I hear babies cry, I watch them grow. They'll learn so much more, than I'll ever know."

Jim stood staring at the house, feeling as if were about to go through another "portal." That's what he was calling them now. The changes in his life that were always preceded by the feeling he now possessed were like doorways, and one thing was for sure, they were unavoidable.

"And I think to myself, what a wonderful world. Yes I think to myself, what a wonderful world."

He climbed the three stairs and knocked hard on the black screen door, not really noticing that the music had stopped.

"I'm blind, not deaf!" he heard from inside the darkened room.

Jim's eyes adjusted. She was sitting in a big rocker not far from the door.

"Ah...Hello, Wilma. It's Jimmy, from across the road. Mom said to..."

"Well cut off my legs and call me shorty!" She interrupted him with a rather deep voice. "Mouse Trap, we've got company."

Something brushed against his leg; it was that calico cat again.

"Well don't just stand there, Jimmy. Come on in!"

He opened the door and the cat shot in ahead of him. "You named your cat Mouse Trap?" he asked, but his words were tentative, as he was still feeling a bit bungling.

"I call that cat a whole mouthful of things, but yes, his name is that all right."

Jim drew his eyes away from the cat, directing them toward the woman in the chair. She wasn't at all what he had expected.

"You're black?" He wished he hadn't said that out loud. Maybe it was her eyes that stunned him. She wore nothing to hide them, and they were pure white. A black woman blinded by the white in her eyes.

The heavyset woman who had been rocking back and forth, back and forth, stopped. Wilma pulled her hands to her face, touching them with one another. "I am? I am? Nobody told me!" She put her hands out in front of her, acting as if she were seeing the color of her skin for the first time. She let out a wail.

"Oh, Lordy! Somebody call the sheriff. There's a Negro in my house!"

"No, no," Jim stammered back, almost dropping the pie. "That's not what I meant at all."

She started rocking again and let out a hearty laugh. "Well, if you aren't as subtle as a horse turd in a cream pitcher."

Jim felt like a fool but she kept right on laughing.

Pushing down hard on the armrests, she stood up, reaching out to touch the wall for guidance.

"Do you want some help?" he offered, noticing the barefoot woman in her simple brown dress with tiny little green buttons. "If I were blind," he thought, "I'd *always* wear shoes."

"Oh, no, I just need to use what I can't see for a little guidance. You understand, don't you?"

Jim didn't answer; instead he just stared at those white eyes of hers.

"I never expected to see you here, child—never ever. Lordy, Lordy. Come, follow me, young Jim Benson, and bring that wonderful-smelling cherry pie with you.

I do declare it has been a long time since I have had your mother's cherry pie!"

Jim looked down at the tin foil. Why had he assumed it was apple?

"Now don't be shy, child. Come right on in."

The cat wrapped around her legs, almost causing her to trip.

"Darn it!" Wilma protested the obstruction. "I'm gonna get me a dog to teach this critter some manners."

The cat let out a big meow and slunk off underneath a large old wooden table that had been stained the color of dark mahogany. Other than the light that came in through the open door between the house and the porch, the room was dark. All of the heavy green floral drapes were pulled shut. The walls were bare, except for what appeared to be a homemade wooden cross near the back door. The rest of the furniture that he could see was sparse as well, and very old. Mary would certainly have liked it.

The room was not unattractive, though; the dark brown wainscot with old-fashioned flowered wallpaper gave the room a feeling of warmth and security. Jim felt very much at ease with this woman, as if he had known her his whole life.

His head whipped in the direction of the curtains. There was something at the top making noises. It was difficult for him to make it out in the dark and the boy crept toward it.

SWOOSH!

Chapter Eight

An object barreled at him, just missing his face and causing him to yell out. It was a bird. The woman took notice of his concern.

"I guess you met my visitor, Jimmy. That darn cat likes to catch birds and bring them in the house and let them go. They like to scare the death out of me!"

Jim was perplexed. "Yes, ma'am." He didn't know what to say to her.

The counter had an old-style radio sitting on top of it. Jim thought that it was a tube type; it must have been the source of the music.

"You sit yourself down at the table while I find us some dishes."

He did as directed. Funny, there were only two chairs, which was uncommon for a piece of this size. She started to hum an old gospel tune that Jim knew well, and his mind filled in the words as her rich voice echoed throughout the darkened room.

"I was standing by my window, on a cold and cloudy day, when I saw the hearse come rollin', for to take my love away. Will the circle be unbroken? By and by, Lord, by and by. There's a better home a-waitin', in the sky, Lord, in the sky."

Wilma's voice was like that of an angel and it lulled him even further into relaxation, as if he were being hypnotized. His boss from Manson, Pedro, used to like to hum this same gospel song. Jim knew without a doubt that Pedro would have loved her voice with its depth and slow, even notes. Closing his eyes, he let her voice carry him with it. Jim found himself humming along, settling an old restlessness inside of his heart.

"*I told the undertaker, 'Undertaker, please drive slow, for this body you are haulin', Lord, I hate to see him go.'*"

Goose bumps rose all along his arms and neck. He was being carried away in his mind again, back to the shack where he had run away.

"No problemo," Jim had replied after Pedro thanked him for the beer.

His friend had come to visit him. How he had found the shack Jim didn't know. It seemed like a lot of his old friends made the four and a half hour drive more than once despite the cold reception they received for their efforts. This visit was no exception and it wasn't long before they were in a bit of an argument. Jim was drunk, of course—had been for hours—and wallowed in self-made misery.

"I want you to listen to me. I want you to hear this. It is something you need to know. See, the thing is, I don't believe in God anymore." Jim had told him, slurring his words.

Pedro's heart was breaking for the man, wondering how his friend could even utter something like that. How could he choose to be so alone?

"Don't say that, amigo. You do not mean those words. You should not say things like that. God did not do this to you." The man watched his friend. "I know that you are angry, but this is life; it is not easy for any

of us. God has other plans. You will see. I tell you the truth."

Jim just waved him off with a hand, taking another drink of the beer, part of it spilling down his beard. "Plans? Listen here a-mee-go, you're wrong, just plain damn wrong. You gonna sit there and tell me that this is God's plan for me? To make me like this? Oh, I know, I'm made in his own image, is that it?" Jim paused, his voice turning ugly. "You see, I prayed and I prayed and I begged! And you know what? There ain't nobody listening. So face it: God isn't there. It's all just a bunch of horse crap."

"How can you say that?"

"'Cause I didn't deserve this. I didn't do nothin' wrong. I tried to live by the commandments as best as I could, okay? The bad things that happen to other people, well, they might deserve what happens to them—I don't know for sure—but not me." He was pointing at himself with his thumb.

"I'm the good one, the one who is supposed to be rewarded, not mutilated. So this is what I figure, Pedro. There is only one explanation that makes any sense. I think God is dead. I think he died just like everything else does. That's why everything is screwed up, 'cause God is dead."

Pedro's mouth dropped open. "Are you loco or something? God isn't dead."

"Then why don't he answer me?" Jim asked while hobbling over to the corner of the trailer to urinate.

"You are upset because every time you snap your fingers, Jesus doesn't appear to cure all of your problems, so you won't believe. You won't believe what you can't see and it makes you angry. Read the Bible. Faith is what healed the sick, not the man himself. Don't you understand? You pray but you don't believe. Praying is not the same as believing."

When Jim was finished, he put his hands over his ears and limped past Pedro toward the house for another beer. He stopped on the porch, looking down on his friend.

"Do you ever ask yourself why? Why do you have to ask for forgiveness or salvation or whatever hell else weakness you need fixed? Why do you have ask? Huh? Why can't your all-powerful God just reach into your pea brain and read your thoughts and just fix it? Why, damn it, do I have to beg like a dog only to have the door slammed in my freaking face? You go back home, preacher, and find someone else to save with your made-up stories, 'cause I've already seen the light. How can anybody be so damn dumb? This life would be a hell of a lot easier if everybody would just see the truth."

Pedro held up a hand. "James," he started, but was interrupted.

"You mean James the Lesser, don't you?"

Pedro looked away, thinking that maybe it had been a mistake to come again. Jim watched him for a second or two longer, but before going in and slamming the

*screen door he added, "Do you know what it feels like
to be nothing more than the firewood for hell?"*

"Everything all right, Jimmy? You seem awfully
quiet over there."

"Yes, ma'am, I'm fine." The sound of her voice
brought him back.

The truth was that Jim was feeling sick to his
stomach at the memory. It made him wonder just how
many of his friends he had hurt. How was he ever going
to reconcile with them? And why Pedro of all people?
He was so good to Jim and in return he had tried to
separate Pedro from God.

FLASH!

Bright blue light filled his brain and Jimmy grabbed
for his chest, the pain so intense that he thought he
might fall from the chair. The room was whirling and
he was spinning into it without control. His eyes
focused for just a moment and he saw people all around
him, strangers. He could hear their voices but not their
words, and blue sky opened up above him where the
ceiling should have been. It was as if part of the room
was outside in another place. Jim felt that he was
starting to lose consciousness when it all stopped as
suddenly as it had begun, just like before.

Jim was sweating and breathing hard, trance-like,
while a thin line of blood dripped from his nose. He
wiped it away without noticing and the clattering of
plates on the table reminded him again of where he
was. Thoughts ran through his head—a dark fear that

maybe there was something wrong with him after all and that maybe his mother should know what was going on. If he died, it would break her heart.

Jim found himself staring down at the plate Wilma had set before him. It was beautiful. In the center was the reflection of his own image and an illusion of a halo around his head. The image was glorious, but Jim felt only pity. Pity for an old blind woman and the wonder of why such beauty was wasted on someone who could not see it.

The chairs were arranged across the table from one another, but Wilma scooted the empty one around to sit right beside the boy.

"My, my, isn't this a wonderful treat? Who would know that today the good Lord would send us such wonderful company and a delightful cherry pie? MMM...MMMM."

Nudging at him with her elbow, she asked, "Would you mind slicing up that pie and serving it?"

Embarrassed, Jim complied. He hadn't even thought of offering to help her; perhaps it was because she was so adept. He was a little clumsy with the utensils, but managed to serve it without making a huge mess.

She fumbled for his hand and held it while bowing her head. "Thank you, Lord, for the gift of food and for the company you have sent a lonely old blind woman."

The cat leapt to the table and stared into Jim's eyes. Jim recognized the look; he had seen it before, and it made him think of a belt buckle. He switched his attention back to Wilma again, then back to the cat.

Chapter Eight

Was she the person in the cat dream? The one who sat on the edge of his bed? Or was she...."

"Meow," the cat cried, startling Jim and breaking his concentration.

Meown' is much like women; the difference is only in the arrangement of the letters. "The arrangement of the letters," Jim was thinking. "The cat's name is Mouse Trap. Her name is W. O. Seyte. There is a connection somewhere in all of this." The boy started to shake.

"Well, of course, I'll share," Wilma said, putting a rather generous piece out for the cat to eat.

"Who are you?" It was a nervous question.

The woman let out another hearty laugh. "Oh, child, don't you know me by now?" She laughed some more. "Just eat some pie. I'm your friend."

Jim didn't move for a moment. There was something he was just going to say to her but now for the life of him he couldn't remember what it was. It had been right on the tip of his tongue. The boy shrugged it off.

Mrs. Benson's pie was incredible, and when they were finished, he helped clean up the dishes before going out into the backyard.

Outside in the bright sunshine, Jim guided Wilma over to a big swinging chair under the maple tree.

"Is it hard to be blind?" He had to ask.

"Is it hard? I don't know. This body has never been able to see. It would be like me asking you: Is it hard to only have two hands, instead of three?"

He could see her point.

"I can see, Jimmy, just differently from you. Everybody sees things differently anyhow."

Wilma paused and rocked the swing a bit, giving Jimmy time to think about what she meant. He figured that it was true. Eyes don't really mean that much to most people, because they don't use them.

"Tell me, friend. What do you see? What is around us? Describe it for me."

He raised his eyebrows and blew out his breath as if he were blowing out the flame of a candle. The question caught him off guard, because he had been looking at her hair instead of listening. Wilma had pretty straight black hair that was nicely styled. It was so perfect that he thought she must have just come back from the beauty parlor, because her blindness wouldn't allow such dexterity.

"I dunno, there are a bunch of trees all around us, and grass that is kind of long. Oh, and over there is a driveway," he said pointing, as if she could follow the point, "and we are facing the back of your house."
Jim didn't know what to say. She didn't know what anything looked like; they were just words to her. She had never seen the shape of a tree, much less the way that it changed colors throughout the year. Wilma had never seen the sky or the sea or the sun. How could he ever begin to describe them to her? There are things in this life that are so stunning that a man can't take his eyes away. The way that a sailor perceives the sea is different from anyone else's point of view. It captivates

him in such a way that the sight never grows old. How could he begin to tell her?

She smiled, rocking a bit more, waiting. He still had the strangest feeling that he knew this woman. Something in his heart told him so, but his head disagreed.

Then, letting him off of the hook, she concluded, "Well, if that is all you see, I have no use for sight."

The boy was embarrassed again. "No, that's not right. I can see these things. I just can't explain them very well. You know what I mean?"

She nodded, the conversation going right where she had expected. "Imagine, Jimmy, describing the spirit of God to the indifferent—to those who cannot see it and therefore have no use for it."

Not even if he had tried to kick and scream his way out of it would Jim have been able to shut out the feelings of his old self that were surfacing within him—feelings that he had refused to experience and had buried right along with his leg. Maybe it was her voice that made him feel this way, or perhaps it was her simple persuasion; either way, she was connecting with him, making him feel loved.

"Do you read the Bible, Jimmy?"

"Used to, when I was a..." Jim almost slipped and said "kid." "Well, no. Not so much anymore."

"Is there a reason?"

"Yeah," Jim thought, "plenty." But it was nothing that he could say to her. Maybe there was a time when he held the sacred book in high esteem, but no longer. After all, it wasn't just a book of salvation; it was also used as the centerpiece on the table of destruction. O'Brien was right: People don't believe in freedom of religion. Everyone has their own idea of how life and death and God all fit together. Their views may have been learned in a church or from a parent, or it may have been something that they just knew was right—but that isn't the problem. The conflict arises because there are those who cannot keep their beliefs to themselves, and they manipulate the Scriptures through interpretation to force their ways upon others. Jim often pondered if it was the thought of either being excluded or separated from a loved one in eternity that drove men mad. He didn't know for sure, but couldn't understand how man, who is so alone by nature, could expect to be anything else in his next change of being.

"Well," he told her, "it's sort of hard to explain."

"Explaining things to someone can be very difficult," Wilma continued. "I have been a teacher for the longest time," she told him while patting him on the leg. "Oh, I've taught all kinds of things to all kinds of people. The hardest thing for all of them to learn is belief. It is as hard for them as it is for me to understand color. I can see belief and I can explain it, but most will not listen. To me they are blind, so I have to find ways so that they can see."

Jim nodded his head up and down, following along with her conversation, enjoying the swing.

"But the color you talk about is there, right? You really do see it? It isn't something that you made up just to tease an old blind woman?"

"Yeah," he said smiling, "it is real."

"Now, I hear that some people cannot see certain colors. They are colorblind, so to speak, but they can still see more than I can. I tell you, Jim, that I do know colors, only differently from you."

Jimmy wrinkled his brow, thinking how she was comparing color to God. Shades of belief? Maybe she was just plain crazy after all, but it was okay; he always did like being around crazy people.

"Now I know that you think it is foolish to say so, but I know the color of the leaves of a tree by the way that they smell and by the way that they sound. I use color as a way to sum up all of the clues."

Jim tilted his head back, still swinging, and gazed upon the bright green young leaves.

"Now, I had to be told that the color of those leaves is a light green. In summer, they become dark green, smelling and sounding much different. I smell them in the fall, when they begin to die, changing again. I know the smell of a yellow daffodil, or a yellow rose or a yellow dandelion. These things I know, but I have never seen them. I think that there are people who *have* seen them, but don't know them the way I do."

Wilma was quiet long enough to let him ponder her meaning. It was relaxing for Jim to be with her, and he was beginning to enjoy being young again.

"Maybe, Jim Benson, if you cannot see belief, you can learn to recognize it some other way."

He turned his head toward her, waiting for her to finish what she meant, but she left him hanging.

Then a question came straight from his lips without consideration. "Wilma, do you think that a person can travel back in time?"

She rocked the swing a bit, a large grin coming to her face, revealing the most beautiful smile. Jim was thinking of another color, purple, and of the one who possessed her same smile, a smile that lights the way for others.

"No, child, you cannot go back to something that you never left. You cannot go in two directions at the same time."

"Never left?" he thought as he watched her. "Crazy, definitely."

"Life is so simple, Jimmy, but rarely does anyone see it. People want to make it complicated and confusing, looking away from the peacefulness. You are alive, because you have been given the gift of experience. Not a single breath is the same as the last. It all changes. It is all different. You are not the person who you left back in time. You changed. But a piece of you stayed there, and you know that this is true because you carry it around in your mind. The experience of that person helped create who you are now. What you choose to experience now will determine what kind of person you will become. In other words, you are merely what your dreams set forth. Would you dare go back and disappoint yourself?

"What you believed that you once wanted to become has changed, has it not? Life is perfect. You are perfect. All you have to do is to open your eyes and see it, then live it."

Jim was scrunching his face again. He meant to tell her that she was wrong, way wrong. He was here back in time, proof that her argument was incorrect.

Then Wilma's voice became quieter, like she was telling a secret to a little child.

"No, you are not here, James. You are only alive in your mind. Everything that you do, everything that you see, everything that you hear isn't real. It is just your imagination."

The hairs stood up on the back of his neck. Had he spoken out loud again or had she understood his thoughts? Maybe he was just confused about what she meant. Whatever the case, he now felt fear and the frustration was evident in his voice.

"Wilma, what are you talking about—only alive in my mind? I'm right here. I'm real, and you're real. How can you say that?"

She was smiling that smile again and he stared at her, very much afraid.

"No, no, child, you are missing it. Look around you again. Don't you see it? This is real; the things in your mind are not. You make up your world with your mind as you go along, planning each step then fulfilling it. If your plan fails in even a tiny way, you become disappointed. You suffer and agonize because you cannot play by your own rules. You refuse to understand that the only thing that matters is that nothing can affect your soul unless you let it. Do you hear me, Jim? This is the power of God—nothing can make you unclean unless you let it.

"Stop making rules, stop planning every little detail, and wake up. Experience your life before it is gone. Everything that you know is temporary. Do you understand? Nothing will last, not even your worst experience. Don't just do things, live them. You sit and breathe without even thinking about it. Take a breath—feel it, smell it, taste it."

Jim closed his eyes to hide from her; she couldn't understand how much pain was in him, pain that couldn't be so easily erased.

"Your body fails because you allow your mind to outgrow it. Is there anything simpler or of greater enjoyment than just honestly experiencing life? Do you see? Do not separate your body from your mind; make them one. Change your thinking. Don't plan, experience. Don't have expectations, have adventures. Some you will like and some you will not, but neither will last. Experience how fast your life is changing and become part of it. Become part of God's spirit.

"When you leave here today to go home, experience the walk—don't just walk. Feel the way your body moves, the way the ground changes under your feet. Listen to it. Enjoy it. Experience your friends and your family before they, too, are gone. Experience your life,

Chapter Eight

Jimmy. It is the easiest thing in the world to do. It is what children do; it is what you once did. Try to remember. Awaken now, child. Your mind has lulled you to sleep from your body."

"I can't do it, Wilma, okay? I just can't do stuff like that."

"And why not? Are you waiting for someone to do it for you? You can, child. I know you. Practice, and whenever you begin to feel like the world is controlling you, just relax and experience it. As you do, you will begin to see what I mean. Let your faith guide you and leave your hate behind. There will always be good things and bad things in your life; it is up to you where you focus your attention. Give your power to the good and let the bad wilt like a plant without water. It is love that will heal you, the love that you give to another. This is the most remarkable experience of all."

The swing had stopped and Jim found himself examining his future-past. He had destroyed his Mary, his family and his life. Pretending to be happy would never fix that. This life would end up no better than his last. He was doomed to be miserable.

"What do you want, child? Tell me."

"I want to be free from myself, Wilma." He turned and looked into her white eyes. "I just want to be released."

"Oh, dear, you be careful what you wish for, Jim Benson. All wishes come true. Don't you know that by now?"

He continued to watch her. "Look, I need to get going."

"Let me give you something."

Jim rolled his eyes, wondering why it was that old people always wanted to give you something when you left. He guided her back into the kitchen where he watched as she wrapped up some cookies in a blue bandanna.

"Take these for your journey, Jim. Perhaps you will find a use for their magic."

Smelling colors and magic cookies; he was going to write a song about this. There was an overwhelming sense of sadness growing within him as he let the screen door slam.

"Come back to me again, young man. There is still time to decide. You know where to find me now."

Jim stopped in the tall grass that wrapped around his legs—as if it were a part of her, trying to hold onto him, to protect him from an unseen corner of his future.

"Wilma?"

"Yes, child?"

"I like your hair."

He couldn't tell if she blushed, but something in her voice let him think so.

"Thank you. It's hard for me to tell if I've done it right."

He turned and let his steps carry him away, but the feelings of sadness did not tag along.

"Everything is beautiful." Jim laughed as he walked down the driveway. "Now that little twirp has got me singing it."

Standing across Shore Road was a man holding his thumb out at an oncoming car. The vehicle that passed between them swerved around the hitchhiker to convey its intentions. Jim noticed that the hitchhiker's appearance was much like his own had been prior to his return to this place in time.

And what of a man's future when it comes to meet his past?

The man dropped his thumb, limping further down the road, leaving what may have been to what may become.

Jimmy snapped back from the illusion and spoke before the stranger was too far away. There was no question in the boy's mind that this man was a vet who hadn't come back from the war—not really.

"Hey," he called while running toward him.

Leery, the man stepped back, but then changed as he saw the light in the young boy's face, the same light that separates men from their weaknesses. They didn't talk at first; the need wasn't there.

"Here, take these." Jim told him, holding out the bandana. "They taste like they're from heaven," he added with a smile.

Wilma was right all along; they were magic. It lay in the way the man thanked him.

Chapter Nine

As Jim was getting ready for bed later that same night, a piece of paper sticking out from his schoolbooks caught his attention. It was the assignment Gilbert had dropped. Jim grabbed it and flopped onto his bed, where he scrutinized it some more. It read:

```
THeMeS
reACH  -ACHIeve,  eXTeND,  SIZe,
TIMe
eXerT - WorK, USe, PoWer, rUN
vIeW -SIGHT, See, ALL, LAND
overDoSe  -  KILL,  USe,  SHoT,
SHADoW
```

"Right on," he laughed, but his laughter was directed more toward himself. Jim was looking at the upper and lower case letters and how they were mixed up— something that he himself used to do and got into trouble for.

"But these aren't random, like mine were. Gil only put e, r, o and v in lower case. Wonder why."

Jim liked letter games. Even in high school, when he had to take those stupid color-in-the-circle tests, he would look for a letter pattern instead of correctly answering the questions. There was a pattern here: four lines with four following words and only four letters in lower case.

"OVER!" he laughed. "It spells over, a four-letter word!" Jim was ecstatic. "But what's the word 'over' got to do with anything?"

His fascination with word games had once led him to the discovery that a handful of writers took the first letter of each paragraph break to spell something out, as if they were saying something else to their readers— like to look for another message, something hidden but nonetheless there.

Then he noticed that the word "over" was not only spelled out with the first letter of each line; "over" could also be used to modify each of them: overreach, overachieve, overextend, and so forth. Gil had even tipped his hand with the word "overdose."

"That 'See Me' teacher missed it. He had had a theme all along!"

He folded the paper back in half, wondering where this would lead, but something told Jim that he might never know. The boy closed his eyes and let the paper fall from his hands onto the floor.

The yelling from her son's room rousted Jim's mom out of bed in the early hours of the morning.

"Honey, wake up! You're dreaming," she told Jim, clapping her hands together.

"MARY! Mary!" he called, his voice frantic.

She shook him. "It's okay, Jim. You're okay. Wake up."

He jerked awake, looking around the room, trying to figure out where he was.

"Are you alright? Who is Mary?" she asked, wondering to herself if this was the same Mary he had been asking for in the hospital—his wife.

"Huh?"

"You were dreaming."

"Is it time to get up?" he asked, still confused.

"You can if you want to," she said standing. "It's a little early still, but we'll be downstairs."

"Okay, Mom."

Mrs. Benson turned and gave him a strange look as she shut the door. He hadn't called her 'Mom' since before the accident.

Jim pulled the pillow out from under his head and gave it a toss. It was soaked in sweat. There hadn't been a single dream that he could remember since he had gotten here, not even the recurring nightmare of the accident could break through. Then again, what would he dream about? Being older? No one dreams of being older, except maybe teenagers in love.

This dream was so real to him, and he replayed everything that he could remember. Jim had been with his wife near their garden in Manson. It was in the springtime and Mary had pushed him out in his wheelchair to get some sun while she planted, occasionally asking him for advice. Already he had grown despondent, replying with little more than grunts. This is what he remembered about the dream: watching his Mary and her garden grow, with her small, caring hands working away.

Then, as if in fast-forward, he saw her again in the fall. Mary was standing in an overgrown patch of weeds and tomatoes and squash, looking out across the lake with a worn face and her arms crossed. Why had she let her garden go?

He called for her by name, but she didn't hear him. Their old dog came up with a nudge, and without hesitating Mary dropped an arm to scratch her behind the ears, but as she did so, the tiny gold crucifix fell from her neck and spiraled into the weeds below—a tent stake in the garden.

"Mary! Mary!" Jim's voice grew louder, but she was turning with the dog and walking away. He tried to push the wheels of his chair to follow but they were wrapped with vines and weeds. "Mary, please wait! Mary, wait for me!" he cried, though she didn't stop.

"COME BACK, MARY!" he screamed at the top of his lungs, but she didn't, and then he woke up.

Jim lay in bed a while longer, looking at the ceiling.

"You can't hear me, can you, Mare? Where are you?" The memory was already leaving him, as real as it was, and with its passing came the feeling that he was losing something.

Jim rolled out of bed and put on some clothes before going downstairs to the kitchen.

"You want a cup of coffee, son?" his father asked.

"Sure, why not."

Mrs. Benson came into the room, rubbing her hands together with hand lotion.

"Do you remember what you were dreaming about?" she asked, still rubbing.

"No, something weird," he lied.

As much as she wanted to pursue it, she didn't. "Don't forget to go over to Eva's after school. Her mom is going to cut your hair."

"I won't."

Mr. Benson set down a cup of coffee in a big blue mug.

"You get out of school at noon today. Is that right?" his father interjected.

"Yep, last day."

"Did you hear anything back from the golf course about that job?" he continued.

"No, I didn't," Jim replied, brightening up, "but I could take the trail back from Eva's and check on it. I kinda forgot all about it with graduation and everything. Are you still going to cook?"

"You bet. I'm going to have you and your brother come in early with me tomorrow. There's quite a lot to do. That okay?"

"Sure, I'm not doin' nuthin'. Oh, wait. I'm on the dance set-up thing, but that's not until around ten, so I can help until then."

"Who are you going to the dance with, son?" Mr. Benson asked.

"I guess I'm going with Eva and Mattie."

"Mattie?" his mother said with a bit of surprise. "Commander Passee's daughter?"

"It's not like a date or nuthin', you know. We're just going as friends."

"You mean to tell me that you are going with *two* girls? That's my boy!" Mr. Benson said, turning back to the big black fry pan with a large grin on his face.

Mrs. Benson gave him a bit of a scowl, shaking her head.

"Now just how did that happen? You and Eva have been planning this for months."

Jack turned toward his wife with a look of his own. For some reason she was always trying to get Eva and Jimmy together.

"I'll tell you, Mom. I don't know just how it happened, but it did. It'll be okay."

She let out a long breath and looked out the kitchen window while her son ate his breakfast.

"Here." Jenny held out a piece of gum for her younger brother. "Now quit bothering me."

"Somethin' bad is gonna happen tomorrow, somethin' real bad...It's Friday the thirteenth, don't cha know?" Danny told them with his eyebrows up as high as he could get them.

"If you tell me that one more time," Jenny said through clinched teeth, "Somethin' bad is gonna happen to you right now."

They had all been waiting at the end of their driveway for the almost empty bus to arrive. As it did, so did a nineteen sixty-eight blue Chevrolet pickup truck, which looked exactly like Old Blue. The truck caught Jim's attention and he hesitated for a moment before stepping aboard the bus, but then went and found his seat without giving it a second thought.

The truth be known, he really didn't recognize it. In fact, Jim no longer knew anything about his future, only his present. It had all vanished with the dream.

Though it may seem odd for a person to lose his entire identity in the course of a few days, it is not at all uncommon for someone to lose it in the course of a lifetime. This is the paradox of life, exchanging who we are for what we want to be. In Jim's case, what would his youth be, coupled with the worries of experience?

After school, Jim found himself sitting in a chair on the back porch of Eva's house, with a green towel wrapped around his shoulders. For the most part it had been rather quiet except for the snipping of scissors and the occasional bird singing. It was very relaxing because Jim loved to get his hair trimmed, especially by a beautiful woman who sometimes brushed her breasts against him.

"So what are you going to do now that school's out, Jimmy?" Eva's mom asked.

Jim was just going to tell her about the golf course job prospect when Eva, who was sitting in a kitchen chair behind her mother, raised her eyebrows up and down in a most provocative way. She was bored and it was starting to show.

"I...I," he stammered, losing his concentration. "I dunno."

Eva bit her lip and opened up her legs just enough to be noticed. Jim felt uncomfortable as it was, but the young girl's antics were making it worse and she seemed to be enjoying every minute of it.

"Are you going to work?"

"Um, yeah, maybe at the golf course as a caddy. I'm supposed to go there on my way home."

"That's good to hear. We'll be seeing a lot more of you then. Did you know that Eva is going to be working there also?"

"No. She is?"

Eva gave him the big okay sign with pretend kisses.

"There, all done. Have a look," Eva's mom told him, holding out a pink hand mirror.

"That looks nice. Thank you, Mrs. Lavenir."

"You are very welcome, young man. I hope you get the job."

"Come on, Jimmy. I want to show you something," Eva said. "Follow me."

"You're gonna get it, girl!" he told her through clinched teeth as they moved away from her mother.

"I hope so."

Jim left the deck and followed his friend across the lawn toward the trail that led back to his house. After a while she stopped and turned toward him.

"So, what do you want to show me?"

She didn't answer him; she just grabbed onto his shirt so that he couldn't move away and began to kiss him.

"Um...ah...what is that all about?"

"I just wanted to know for myself," she said in a hushed voice, having not moved very far from his face, "what your girlfriend already knows."

"Oh."

"Is that okay?"

"Sure," he whispered, allowing himself to be seduced.

"Jim," she said, pushing him away, "you are going with me, right? Mattie is coming, but we're together now, right?"

"Yes," he answered, falling under her spell.

"Then tell me."

"I'm with you, Eva."

"Good," she told him while putting her arms around him and pulling him back tight against her body.

Still on cloud nine, Jim had made it to an old pond along the trail home when he was startled by a voice from the trees.

"What you doin' here, Jim Benson? You ought not be here. This ain't your place. You go home. They're callin' you. Go."

Jim froze at the sound of the deep, menacing voice. "What? Who's there? Come out."

From out of an old oak tree dropped Gilbert. He was wearing a pair of bib overalls and no shirt. In his right hand he held an ax. "Go home from here. Go now, afore it's too late."

"What are you talkin' about, Gil? I'm goin' home, from Eva's. What are you doin' with that ax?"

"Cuttin' wood for Mother," he answered. He stretched the tool out and pointed to a rather large stack of split wood.

Relief swept through Jimmy.

"Mother says sometimes folks just need to be told things outright. I'm tellin' you outright: You go home."

Jim was getting nervous as the man-boy approached and if he hadn't been so scared he might have noticed that Gil's eyes were no longer crossed.

"Don't get weird on me, man. I just told you I was on my way. Let me by. I'm goin' that way to the golf course," he tried to say as well as he could.

Gil didn't move from the fork in the trail. "You don't hear good, do you? That ain't the way home. You go that way," he said, pointing with his free hand to the other trail.

"I'm goin' to see about a job, okay? Just let me go by."

Chapter Nine

Gil threw the ax down to the ground as he came toward Jim. "You git outta these woods now. You don't know the way. You run—now! Afore it's OVER, JIM! YOU HEAR ME?" he screamed. "AFORE IT'S OVER. RUN!"

Jim started to scamper backwards and ended up falling, but before he could get up Gilbert was leaning over him, screaming at the top of his lungs.

"WHAT'S THE MATTER WITH YOU? DON'T YOU GET IT? YOU GOTTA CHOOSE OR YOU'RE GONNA HAVE TO STAY HERE. I SAY RUN, BOY!"

Jimmy rolled around trying to shield himself from the dirt Gilbert was kicking at him.

"GO HOME. GO HOME. GO HOME. FOLLOW THE VOICES!"

"Gilbert! That's enough. He doesn't understand. Leave him alone."

The man-boy stopped and backed away. "Yes, Mother."

She sauntered up to the boy lying on the ground. "So here you are after all," she said, and took a swig from the bottle of beer she was holding.

"Look at you, crawling around in the dirt like a bug. Stand up!"

Jimmy jumped to his feet, terrified.

"What are you so afraid of? Ain't no one here gonna hurt you. What are you doing here?"

"I was going home from Eva's house. That's all."

"Eva? Why that's Gil's girl. Ain't that right, son?"

Gil nodded with a big yellow grin.

"What you messin' with his woman for?"

Jim was starting to think that she was as crazy as her son when her face lit up in one of the most pleasant smiles he had ever seen.

"I'm just teasing you, Jimmy. You know that," she said with a wink toward Gil, who put a hand over his face to hide a giggle. Jim watched as she tilted her head back and shook her long hair, then scratched at her rear through a worn housedress that wasn't all the way buttoned. She let out a long breath and took another drink of beer before continuing, "You seem like a smart one to me. Are you?"

Jim shrugged, feeling less afraid. "I guess."

"Well, you can go by us and up that path if you want. We won't stand in your way."

"Why shouldn't I?" he asked, but his attention was focused upon a small gold cross that was just visible through the close-to-transparent dress.

"Because it would be the wrong way. Didn't you hear Gil?"

"Yeah, but I'm not going home."

She let out a long sigh and studied him for a moment. "Close your eyes, son. Go on, close them."

Jim watched her, debating whether or not to listen to her, then did as she asked.

"Now listen. Just listen to each of your choices."

Jim couldn't concentrate. He kept thinking that Gil was going to throw something at him and tried to keep one eye a little opened.

232

"Trust me."

He opened the eye a little more, then closed it all the way.

"Where does the sound come from, Jim?"

"All around me."

"No. You listen but you don't hear. Where does the sound come from?"

He stood quiet for the longest time, until he started to sway, and then he heard it. "That way. It's that way," he said with some excitement in his voice, pointing toward the path home and not the way that he had wanted to go.

Jimmy opened his eyes and looked down the trail that he was pointing towards then back toward Gil's mother, but she and her son were gone.

"Hello? Mrs. DeDana? Gil?" He felt scared again, like there was something else in the woods with him, something dark. "Come out," he called, but they didn't and the fear grew into terror. Jim turned and started to run with everything he had down the path home.

It was the better part of a mile before he finally stopped running. Gilbert was big and weird anyway but the stories that went around town made him all the scarier.

"They are just crazy. That's all. Just crazy," Jim kept telling himself. Most of the kids wouldn't go past the old pond because they were afraid of running into "Screaming Gil" or his alcoholic mom. Besides, it didn't make any sense what she was talking about.

Then it dawned on him; the rumor was that she had a whiskey still hidden in the woods and that's what Gil must have been cutting the wood for.

"I'm so dumb. I hope that I'll still be able to get that job."

Jim was walking down the path, still muttering to himself, when he heard girls' voices coming from what would one day be Mary's house. He got down on his hands and knees and crept along the back of the stone wall to spy on the visitors. As he got behind the house, he stopped to try to hear what they were saying, but the voices were still muffled. He raised his head above the wall for a better look, only to stare into the golden eyes of an old sheep dog.

"WOOF! WOOF!"

"Son of a…!" Jim leapt to his feet, spinning away and yelling some more.

A girl in the upstairs window stuck her head out, calling her dog. Jimmy also tried to pacify the animal, though he was now red faced.

"Is that you, Jimmy Benson?"

Jim squinted back. He knew her—she was one of Jenny's friends from upstate. This was her father's summer home.

"Yeah, it's me," he said, looking down at his trousers to make sure he hadn't peed his pants or something.

"I never heard you yell like that before. You scared of that old blind dog?"

"I was yellin' cause I saw it was you, Karen. That's all."

They grinned at one another.

"You guys here for the summer already?" Jim's dialect had changed without him knowing it. Now he had an accent and "summer" sounded like "summah."

She flipped her short red hair from side to side, wanting to make sure Jim took notice of her new and improved bust line. He did.

"Nah, my dad is introducing his friend to somebody in the shipyard, and I just tagged along to get out of St. John for a while. We have to leave on Saturday, but Dad says we'll be back in a few weeks. Is Jenny home?"

"I don't know. She might be out with Greg."

"Greg?"

"Yeah, some new guy she's been seeing. He's cool."

Karen did the flip thing again. "Maybe we could double with them some time?"

Jim was shaking his head no; she was always after him. New improved bust line or not, Jim had been warned by his father early on about redheads.

"You stay away from them," he had said. "Their taste is like honey, their smell is like flowers, and they will lure you and captivate you until you can never escape. Then, when they take you to bed they will wear you out to nuthin', son. Ever see a man who is married to one? He looks tired, damn tired."

Nope. Redheads scared Jim. He didn't want to go through life looking damn tired.

From within the house, Jim could hear a man's voice calling, "Supper is ready, girls!" He wondered if it was really that late already. How long had he been in those woods?

Karen turned and yelled, "Coming." Then leaning back out the window again, she said, "I gotta go, pretty boy. Have Jenny give me a call, would ya? Oh, wait. Never mind. The phones aren't on yet. Just tell her I'll catch up with her later."

She blew him a kiss but Jim just waved it off and turned to walk away, avoiding the old dog. Karen disappeared from the window, but in the shadows of the room another girl stayed and stared after the boy who was still visible through the trees.

Karen stopped at the top of the stairs to call for her friend. "Come on, Mary. Let's go."

There were lots of things that Jim was going to do this summer, but right now he was doing his favorite, lying on the lawn and looking at the sky.

"Oh, yoo-hoo, Jimmy!"

Jim closed his eyes for a second, hoping it would make Karen go away.

"Hey, frog." He was insulting her because she was from a French family.

"Call me that again and I'll jump you," she told him, coming closer with a smile. "Who knows, though. I might anyway."

Jim jumped to his feet.

"Chicken."

She had on a black velvet choker, something Jim hadn't noticed before. In fact, he thought, she was pretty well dolled-up for a girl who was just on a "visit." Karen flipped her sassy hair and gave Jim a wink, causing him to blush and look down at his feet.

The screen door slammed as Jenny came out. "Karen!" she screamed with excitement. Karen took a few steps up the hill to give her friend a hug, but Jim was now watching the girl who had been standing back.

"Hi," she said, and held out a hand toward Jimmy. "I'm Mary."

"Hey," he said, taking her hand. "Jim." Pictures of this girl suddenly flashed through his mind. It was as if he could see her growing old.

He must have appeared somewhat strange because she asked if he was all right.

"Yeah," Jim replied, snapping out of it and letting go of her. "I just felt weird for a second. Sorry. I think I've seen you before somewhere. You live around here?"

Mary bit her lower lip and shook her head back and forth. "No, this is my first time to Cape Neddick. I live up in St. John. My dad is here looking at a job in the shipyard."

She wore no makeup of any kind, or nail polish or even jewelry. Mary stood there as she was in a simple white blouse, a pair of well-worn denim jeans and white sneakers. Jim nodded, taken in by her captivating beauty, trying to think of something to say. "Are you guys out of school already?"

"No, we just skipped."

He shrugged when Karen interrupted their conversation. "Mary, come meet Jenny."

She turned away from Jim, her body moving well before her eyes did, and followed the command.

"You guys wanna come up to my room?" Jenny asked. "I've got a new 45."

"Coming with us, Jimmy?"

"No thanks, Karen. I'm going down to the beach for a while."

"Beach?" Mary lit up. "How far is it?"

"Just down that trail," he said, pointing without looking. "Not very far. You can come if you want."

"Okay."

"You thinkin' of movin' in on my man, Mare?" Karen said with a smile, noticing that Jimmy had rolled his eyes.

Mary said something to her in French and Karen answered right back, causing them both to laugh hysterically. Karen whispered into Jenny's ear to let her in on the joke.

"Come on. Let's go," he said, somewhat red faced. He hated it when girls made fun of him, in any language.

Mary gave him a little salute behind his back and winked at Karen as she followed, still smiling and swinging her arms in a pretend march.

"Don't do anything that I wouldn't do!" Karen cried.

Mary turned around and gestured. "Yeah? Name something that you wouldn't do, Karen."

A ways down the trail Jim had to ask, "So what were you guys saying back there?"

Mary giggled. "I told her that maybe I wanted to keep you."

"Really?" Jim said while walking backwards to check her sincerity and sort of hoping it was true. "And that was what was so funny?"

"No, Karen said that I could have you because your butt is too skinny to give her a good push."

Jim turned back around and kept walking, his face reddening again. "I'd be a good pusher," he thought to himself, but part of him wasn't exactly sure what she meant.

"Is that an apple tree? I love apple trees," Mary said, cutting through the woods toward an old red house with a manicured tree.

Jim hesitated before following.

"I dunno what it is."

"It's an apple tree. See all of the little baby apples?"

Jim could see her again in his mind, surrounded by hundreds of trees, but she was much older. A big man with a tan face was singing to her while thinning the fruit.

"Don't sit under the apple tree with anyone else but me, anyone else but me, anyone else but me. Don't sit under the apple tree with anyone else but me, 'til I come marching home." Mary started throwing them at him. "You better not go marching off any place, mister!" The man laughed and ducked around the tree

to grab her, pulling her down to the ground. "Stop it, you pervert. Leave me alone!" But she wrapped her arms around him and pulled him tight.

"Hey! Space cadet! You in there?" she asked, waving a hand in front of his face.

Jim jumped back and looked at her again, still not speaking.

"What's wrong, Jim?"

"Nothing, I guess. You like your eggs with ketchup, don't you?"

"How did you know that?"

"I don't know. It's like a part of me thinks it knows you, but it's not you—it's an old you."

"What?"

"Never mind. I got hit in the head last week, and things have been sort of weird since then. Sorry."

She headed back toward the path. "Am I pretty when I'm old?" She stopped and waited for an answer.

"No," he said softly. "You're pretty now. When you are old, you are beautiful."

Mary's cheeks turned pink. "I knew I wanted to keep you," she said, and ran ahead of him.

Standing side by side where the trail opened up into the salt breeze, the two of them watched the waves crash into the rocks, changing them from blue to white.

Mary sniffed the air and looked at Jim with a smile.

"Look at these rocks!" she told him with excitement in her voice. "They look like all of the layers of the earth turned up on their side."

"Yeah, pretty cool, huh? There's some deep pools down that way," he said, pointing, "that fish get trapped in during the tide change. Sometimes I fish for them, but there are also lots of starfish and other stuff to look at."

"Can we go down closer that way?" she asked, pointing to a channel in front of them that yielded an occasional splash.

"Sure. Follow me."

Down the giant steps they went, Mary pausing every once in a while to accept Jim's hand for balance. At the bottom, they sat along the edge of a channel with their feet dangling over the side.

"Does it ever get rough here?"

"Yeah, but usually not this time of year. Pappy brought all of us down here last winter. We had to walk through the snow and it was so rough that you couldn't leave the woods or you would get wet."

Mary looked behind her some fifty yards upward. "Wow, that's a long ways."

Jim nodded. "It was so loud when the waves would crash you thought for sure that they were going to grab you. Sarah even started to cry because she was so scared."

She looked around for a while, sometimes holding a hand to her eyes to shield them from the sun. "This is nice, Jim. You are lucky to live in a place like this."

Jim nodded. "Yeah."

"Do you ever come here to watch the sunrise?"

"No. Pappy and Mom do, though, every once in a while."

"I'll bet it's beautiful. Too bad we couldn't watch the sunset. Guess we are on the wrong coast, huh?"

Jim smiled. He liked the way she talked in a singsong voice.

"Is that a lobster boat?"

"Yeah, out of Ogunquit, I'd guess. He'll come in real close and get those pots."

Jim was thinking of something else to say when Mary reached over and took hold of his hand. Whatever thoughts he had were now quieted. Now he wanted nothing more than to just stay here with her.

"This is nice," she told him. "I'd come here every day if I lived here."

"If you lived here, I'd come with you every day."

Mary turned and looked into his eyes. "Why are you here now, Jim?"

He sort of shrugged. "Because you're here."

"I'm going to leave, you know."

"I know."

"Everyone is going to leave."

"You sound kinda sad the way you said that. What do you mean?"

Mary didn't answer him immediately, and looked away, asking, "What is it that you like about being alive?"

"That's the kind of thing a hippie chick would ask."

"I'm serious, Jim."

"Oh," he sat for a moment, thinking about it. "Having a body. That's what I like. And I don't care if somebody else doesn't think it's perfect either—it's mine. I like it just the way it is."

"What if it quit working right. What then?"

"Mean like when I'm old or somethin'?"

"Or what if you just got sick...or hurt?"

"Dunno. Guess I'd still feel the same, but I don't know for sure."

"Do you ever think about dying, Jimmy?"

"Not really. Why? Have you?"

"I never used to, but sometimes it is all I *can* think about." She let go of his hand and rubbed the palms of her hands across her knees.

"What's wrong?"

"My mom. She's really sick. The doctors said she has cancer."

"Oh, she smokes?"

"No, it's a different kind. Something is wrong with her bones and she is going to die."

Jim didn't know what to say and tried to imagine what it would be like if he knew his mom was going to die. He didn't like the idea.

"Did she come with you?"

"Mom? No. Dad said she needed some time alone."

"I'm sorry to hear that, Mary. I don't know what I'd do if I knew one of my parents was going to die."

"Well," she said hesitantly, "first you cry. You cry until you realize that it doesn't do any good, but that takes a long time. Then you start remembering all of the things that you used to do with them, but that doesn't help either. That just makes you sad, 'cause then you start thinking what your life will be like when they are gone."

She grew quiet and Jim watched the breeze blow her long blond hair back and forth across her shoulders.

"Then all of a sudden you figure it out, and it's not so bad."

"What do you figure out?"

She turned and got close to him, close enough that he could feel her breath. Jim's heart began to race.

"You figure out that thinking about the past or imagining the future is a waste of time because it steals from you. It steals the present, and that is the only time that you can really be with somebody else."

"I don't get it."

She put one hand around his neck and pulled him even closer and kissed him.

"Wake up," she whispered. "Don't go."

Jimmy became confused. "I'm not going anywhere."

"Wrong," she countered, and pushed away from him. "Every time you think of either the past or the future, you leave. You leave the present, and when you do you miss it."

"Miss what?"

"You miss your life. Look, all the time I spent crying and feeling sorry for myself I could have spent with my mom. I wasted it and I can't get it back. So now I just pay attention to everything that is going on in my life, and you know what? I don't regret the past as much and I don't worry about the future. Do you understand?"

Jim nodded, watching her green eyes sparkle.

"You need to stay where it is real."

"I could probably do that."

"It means that you have to be the person that you are, not somebody that you think you were or somebody you're going to be. It's hard because things change and you have to be willing to change with them. Except," she said, pausing, "except they'll come for you. They always come. The past will bring with it wonderful lies it calls memories while the future will invent a world from your dreams. The present is your only truthful friend because it doesn't try to convince you what to believe—that's your choice. When they do come for you, Jim, think of me. I'll help you remember. Don't let them take you."

"Let who?"

"The past and the future. They'll fight for you."

"Mary? Has anyone ever told you that you are just a little, well…"

Before he could finish the sentence, she grabbed him again and playfully kissed him. "Told me what?" she asked, and kissed him again. "Huh?" And again. "I'm beautiful when I'm old? Yes, Jim, you have!" And she pushed him back onto the rocks where she allowed her body to fall upon his.

A strong wave crashed into the inlet, splashing the two of them.

"Yikes!" Mary said, trying to cover herself up.

"We should get back a ways. Sometimes it can get pretty rough."

They stood up, and as Jim turned around Mary slipped over the side without a sound, plunging into the deep channel. Within seconds the water had sucked her out to sea.

"We could go up the beach to the rock if you want," he said, turning back toward her, but she was gone.

"Mary?" he said, looking all around.

She surfaced some thirty feet from shore and screamed.

"MARY! SWIM OUT! SWIM OUT! I'M COMING."

The boy panicked, knowing that if a wave caught her it would slam her body into the jagged shoreline. He scampered down the rocks to the edge, where he dove into the frigid water and began to swim out towards her, but as he neared, a wave swept the girl away from him.

"NO! SWIM AWAY FROM IT!" he called, but it was too late and the ocean heaved her tiny body towards the shore.

Jim began to swim with everything he had, but to no avail. But instead of killing Mary, the wave somehow just lifted her above the rocks and left her sitting unscathed on a seaweed bed. She jumped to her feet and climbed to the safety of the next-highest platform.

"I'm okay! I'm okay!" she hollered, waving an arm.

Relief swept through Jim but only until another wave slammed into his head. The cold water was already taking effect and he knew that if he didn't find a way out soon, he would drown.

The *Isidore* had taken notice of the boy in the water and turned hard starboard, sounding its horn. Jim waved his arms frantically.

FLASH!

Bright blue light filled Jim's brain, making his body go limp. He disappeared from the water's surface, sinking into the depths below.

Imprisoned by the sea, the boy began to hear his name being called by muffled voices that seemed to be getting farther and farther away. Through the water he could see the outline of something white coming toward him.

"Oh, God," he thought, terrified, "what is it?"

Jim was floating above a room and could see an angry bearded man wearing an eye patch screaming at a woman.

"THEN I'M LEAVING! I DON'T NEED YOU ANYMORE!"

"Don't you leave, Jim. Don't you dare walk out on us." It was Mary. She was crying.

"She called him 'Jim,'" he thought. "That's me...no, it can't be...she's talking to me!"

"How long has it been?" another voice boomed.

"I don't know."

"Well, we're going to try. Help me."

Now the captain's hand pierced the water and grasped onto Jim with all the strength he could muster. The deck hand, a girl no older than Jim, grabbed onto him as well.

"I gotcha, kid. Hang on!"

They pulled Jimmy up the side of the boat and onto the deck, where he lay like a lifeless fish. The man pushed hard onto Jim's stomach, then grabbed and lifted him by the top of his jeans and pushed again.

"Wreeetch." Jimmy threw up salt water and rolled to his side, gasping for air.

The captain let him go and bolted up the ladder to the bridge to maneuver the vessel away from the shore before it crashed.

The engine roared with full power as the prop turned in reverse. The girl, dressed in yellow bib rain gear and boots, watched Jimmy cough himself up off of the deck and to the boom that still supported a swinging lobster trap.

As the stern passed within inches of the shoreline the captain began to yell, "JUMP! JUMP NOW! GO ON, BOY!"

He turned and looked up to the bridge, disorientated. The man's huge arm pointed aft.

Mary was also yelling, "Jump, Jimmy. Jump."

Jimmy took his chance and leapt over the side of the ship, sprawling out across the rocks, cutting his knees.

He made his way to his feet and followed Mary's voice to safety. With blue lips and chattering teeth, Jim waved at the strangers in the boat, who in turn blew the horn and went back about their routine of pulling traps as if nothing had happened.

"Oh, your nose is bleeding, Jimmy. Are you okay?"

"Yeah," he answered, his voice shaking from the cold, "I'm fine." He rubbed his hand across it to see how bad it was.

"That was so scary. I thought you were going to drown."

Jim looked into her eyes, feeling as if he were going to collapse. "I thought the same about you."

He bent over to look at his knees. They hurt and his throat was on fire.

"You're okay now," she said with a little nod, putting her hand on his shoulder. Her touch quieted his fears.

"You came in after me. Thank you."

"Sure."

"I'm freezing," she chattered.

"Me too. Come on. Let's go back. It'll warm us up."

Just as they entered the trailhead Jimmy stopped and glanced back, but to his surprise, the *Isidore* was nowhere in sight.

"Hurry! Faster!" Mary pushed behind Jim, giggling. Minutes later the two of them came across the lawn, only to be stopped by Jim's mom.

"You're all wet! Why are you all wet?" she demanded, but her attention was on the little blonde with the now see-through white blouse. Mrs. Benson hadn't seen her around before.

"We had an accident and," Jim started, but then paused, noticing for the first time the way the shirt stuck to Mary's skin. It was very revealing.

Mary wondered what they were staring at and looked down, which caused her to scream and cover herself. Jim's mom was preparing to continue her interrogation when Karen stepped out on the porch.

"Mrs. Benson, um, Jenny needs you right away. She's pretty upset."

"Upset? Why? What's wrong?"

"Um. That guy she's been kind of going out with, um, Greg. Well, he called just now and told her that he got his letter and has to report in two weeks. He says he's gotta go to Vietnam."

"Oh, dear. Jim, go get some dry clothes on. Both of you. Go on."

She left and Karen came closer. "Why are you guys all wet?"

"Long story," Mary said, walking past, arms still folded across her chest.

"Bye, Mary," Jim hollered after her. "I like your shirt," he said, laughing, feeling more like himself again.

"Pervert!" she turned around and told him while still walking backwards, then for fun raised her hands above her head and shook her chest at him.

"Come back!" he yelled but she didn't; she only turned and ran away.

"You are such a tramp, Mary!" Karen said, giggling.

"Only for the right guy, and…he is the right guy."

"Wow," Jim said aloud, watching the two of them disappear. "Wow, wow, wow." He went into the house to change.

Chapter Ten

Early Friday morning Mr. Benson got his two boys out of bed, fed them breakfast and ushered them off to the school cafeteria where they spent their time peeling potatoes, chopping vegetables and doing other assorted kitchen tasks.

"Um, Pappy?"

"Yes, Jim."

"It's almost ten, and I'm supposed to be over at the gym to help set up for the dance."

"Right-o. Thank you for your help."

Jimmy took off his white apron and started heading out the door when he noticed the grim expression on his little brother's face.

"Hey, Pappy?" he yelled to be heard over the other kitchen helpers. "Danny is supposed to come with me."

Mr. Benson waved a hand while Danny's face exploded in a smile.

"Come on. You can blow up balloons with that helium stuff," he said with a wink, remembering what it was like to be ten years old.

After entering the gymnasium from the short hallway, Jim noticed that Mattie was standing just inside the door.

"Hey, Jimmy," she bubbled.

"Hey yourself," he said, stopping.

Danny stopped as well, but Jim pointed him to the balloons over by the stage.

"We haven't really had a chance to talk about tonight. It's okay if you don't want to go with me, you know. Maybe I got the wrong impression."

"Who said that? I'll meet you out in the lobby right after graduation."

"Are you sure?" she asked, coming closer. "I don't want to make trouble between you and Eva. I think she kind of likes you."

"Yeah, I'm sure. I already got the tickets. We used to have a lot of fun together. I just sort of messed it up. Besides, me and Eva are just friends."

Mattie had moved dangerously close to him and the magic spell she cast was starting to take effect.

"Did you mean all of those things that you said in the woods?"

"Uh huh," he responded, but he was having trouble concentrating; she smelled so good. What had he said to her that day? It now seemed foggy.

"I got a new dress."

Chapter Ten

"Yeah? For tonight?"

"Yeah," she whispered, "you'll like it. We should go someplace where we can talk in private."

"JIM!" Eva screamed from across the room. "Get over here." He knew by the tone in her voice that she was getting ready to get mean.

"Oh, um, I gotta go to work. I'll ah…" But he didn't finish the sentence. He just smiled and backed up.

Eva moved her attention from Jim to Mattie and gave her a "look."

Halfway between the two girls the doors to the outside of the building opened up, filling the entire room with bright sunlight. Jim turned toward it, squinting and trying to see who was coming in. As his eyes adjusted he could see it was a girl, but not just any old everyday girl. It was Mary.

FLASH!

The room started to spin, and the boy grabbed his chest, yelling out before falling straight to the hardwood floor. His head hit it with a resounding thump and Jimmy was out cold.

Eva and Mattie screamed and started running toward him but Mary stood where she was, almost as if she had expected this all along.

They were around him now, pulling on him. Somebody had leaned over to block the sun from getting into his eyes, and though he couldn't see the man's face, he could see the blue sky above them. Another man leaned over and they started talking.

"You got him?"

"Yeah. Help me with his head."

"Is he breathing?"

"Not well enough. Tilt his head back."

"Wipe that blood off his nose or he'll choke to death."

"Does anyone know his name?"

"His name is Jim. Jim Benson," a voice from the crowd said.

"Jim? Jim? Can you hear me, Jim? You're gonna be okay. Just hang in there."

"This doesn't look good. How long has it been?"

"Just do your job."

"Jim? Jim?"

"Damn it. You're gonna have to hit him. CLEAR."

FLASH!

Virtually every nerve in Jimmy's body screamed out with pain as his back arched up off of the gym floor. The two male teachers who were leaning over him tried to steady him. One of them had been slapping the side of his face.

"Make a hole." The voice was unmistakable. Danny had gone straight for their father as soon as he saw what had happened.

"What's going on here?"

"I seen it all," a kid said, stepping into view. "He fainted and his head hit the floor. He got knocked out. I seen it happen before in football."

Jimmy's eyes came back into focus and he sat up, holding his nose.

"You okay, son?"

"Yeah, Pappy."

"Here. Hold this on your nose until the bleeding stops," he offered, holding out a white handkerchief. "How's your head?"

Jim took the cloth with one hand and rubbed the back of his head with the other. "Smarts."

"What happened?"

Jim glanced around, looking at the faces until his eyes stopped on Eva. Funny, he could have sworn that there was a firefighter leaning over him, but where did he go? Eva's face looked pale.

"I dunno. Guess I fell again or somethin'. I'm okay now." He smiled.

A wave of relief swept through the small group that had crowded around him.

"Look," he said, showing the handkerchief to his father. "The bleeding has already stopped."

Jack Benson let out a long sigh. "Son, you're gonna drive me to drinkin' if I have to take you to the emergency room one more time. It's a damn good thing your mother isn't here to see this. Think you can stand up?"

"Yes, sir."

Jim got to his feet with no apparent side effects.

"Come on. You're coming with me back to the mess hall where I can keep an eye on you."

Jim followed behind his father when he remembered that he had seen Mary. He turned around to look for her. Out of all of the faces that were still looking at him, hers was not one of them.

"Huh," he grunted as he turned and walked away.

Jim no sooner sat down on a stool in the cafeteria than his mother's car pulled up to the open back door.

"Go help your mother unload, Jim."

While he lugged in boxes and trays covered in tin foil, his parents had words just out of earshot. Not that it mattered, because he had heard it all before. They were discussing another one of his "accidents."

"Come on, honey. You are coming home with us."

"Mom, I said I would help," he protested.

When his father started his way, Jim turned and gave in, climbing into the back seat behind his little sister.

"Are you in trouble?" she asked, poking her blue eyes above the seat.

"No."

"Then why are you here?"

"Turn around or else."

Sarah turned around. Jim could be a bully when he wanted to. His mom got into the car and adjusted her rearview mirror so she could see him. He contemplated moving across the seat but thought better of it.

"Are you alright?"

"Yes."

"Your father said you fainted."

Jim was wishing that she would either start the car or at least turn around and face him. He hated the mirror interrogation routine.

"I just fell," he told her, turning his head to look out the side window.

"He told me that you couldn't get up."

"I got up, just not right away."

"Uh-huh." She waited, still staring. "What about your nose?"

"It quit bleeding a long time ago."

"You need to be more careful or one day you are going to get hurt bad."

Jim turned and looked back into the mirror to dispute her, but she had turned around. The way she held her eyes on him told Jim that she wasn't scolding him. She was concerned.

"I'll be more careful," he said, holding her eyes with his. "Promise."

Satisfied, Jane Benson started her station wagon and the three of them rolled their way out of the Cape Neddick High School parking lot toward home.

Even though Jim didn't feel tired, he took his mother's suggestion after lunch and went upstairs to his room to lie down on his bed. Two and half hours later, he woke up to find his pillowcase covered in blood.

"Son of a…" he said after rubbing a hand across his nose.

He got up and flipped over his pillow and went down the hall to wash off his face. Jim was pretty sure that if his mom found out, she might not let him go to the dance. On his way out of the bathroom, he heard the phone ringing and picked it up in the hall.

"Hello," he said into the yellow wall phone.

"Hi, Jimmy. Its Eva. Are you okay?"

"Yeah, I'm fine."

"You need to be more careful."

"Nag, nag, nag."

"Are we still going tonight?"

"Yep. What time do you want to meet?"

"I wanted to know if you could come to graduation with us. We could pick you up on the way."

"Okay." He liked the idea of going with her better than riding with the "folks."

"There's an all-night party afterwards for the graduates, but we could sneak in," she whispered. "It would be fun."

Jimmy's head was swimming with excitement. "Yeah? I'll ask, but they'll probably let me. What time are you coming?"

"Um, hold on."

Jim turned and leaned against the wall, fidgeting with the door handle that led up into the attic. He gave the door a pull and looked up the short stairwell. In his mind, there was a little blonde calling his name. It was Mary, only she seemed a few years older.

"Come on," she told him, smiling and holding a finger to her lips. Jim could see himself following the illusion, as if it were a memory, and climbed into the stifling hot air, looking around to try to see where she had gone.

"Over here. This way."

Chapter Ten

She was standing across the room, then disappeared through another door that led to a small bedroom that may have at one time been a servant's quarters. Once through the doorway he could see her lying on her back on one of the double beds.

"Close the door and come here."

He did as he was told and sat down beside her. A cool breeze coming through the open window relaxed him.

She rubbed a hand across his leg. "I love you, Jim Benson."

Swallowing hard, he smiled. "I love you, too."

"Yeah?"

"Yeah. More than you'll ever know."

"Then come here," she whispered.

Jim, more than a little nervous, complied. He lay next to her, his hand sneaking its way up the inside of her green shirt.

SLAP! "Pervert! Whaddya think yer doin'?" she asked with a giggle.

Jim was embarrassed and it showed on his face.

"What? Did you think that we were going to...?" She giggled some more, raising up her eyebrows. Waiting, then, "Oh, quit pouting. Here," she said, taking a hold of his hand and putting it back where it had been. "Just a little, okay? But don't start drooling on me."

Jim smiled, glad to be back in the game.

"Listen, I want to tell you something. So just don't say anything until I spit it out, okay?"

Jim nodded, concerned at the way her voice had changed to a whisper. He stopped the advance of his hand and looked into her emerald eyes that were but inches from his.

Mary was silent for a moment, lost in her thoughts, before beginning again in her hushed manner. "When I was a little girl I used to always dream of meeting the perfect guy. Maybe all little girls do. I used to think about the way that he would look and act and," she paused and smiled, "even smelled. But I never knew how he would make me feel. I mean, I thought that I would be in love and he would love me and we would be happy, you know? Then one day I meet him. I meet you." She swallowed and kissed him. "Well, you don't look anything like you're supposed to—not even close. But you smell good, and the way that you make me feel…it just makes me want to be with you, always. You are a beautiful person inside, and that's what I love about you."

She didn't have to worry about Jim interrupting. He was speechless.

"So," she said, grinning again, "are you going to get busy with that hand or what?"

"Jim?"

Eva's voice brought him back into the hallway. "Dad says we can be there in an hour and a half. I'm so excited about tonight. Call me back if you can go to the party, okay?"

"Yeah," he stuttered, "I will." But suddenly he felt guilty for just being on the phone with her.

He hung up and stared up at the attic and though he tried to shake it off as he went back to the bedroom, he felt more than ever that he needed to see that little blond-haired girl, and soon.

"No."

"Mom, everyone's gonna be there."

"No, you're not going, Jim. The party is for the graduates. I want you home right after the dance. Is that clear?"

"Fine. I'll be outside."

"Don't wander too far. It's almost time to get ready."

Jim let the black screen door slam behind him and walked down the driveway toward the mailboxes. Thunderclouds rolled over his head, blocking out the sun. Coming down the driveway to meet him was Wilma, complete with a seeing-eye cat.

"Hi, Wilma."

"Is that you, young Jim Benson?"

"Yes, ma'am."

"Well, you saved me a walk. Here. I brung you back your mother's pie platter. You be sure and tell her for me how much I love her cookin'."

"Okay."

"Are you alright, child? You sound down to me."

"I'm fine."

Distant thunder rolled its way toward them, causing them both to look up. The sky was turning black as the storm approached.

"Angels is talkin' now. Best be gettin' ready."

"What angels, Wilma?" Jim sort of smirked.

"Them ones that's around you, child, all around you."

"What, so they like follow me around watching my every move?"

"Oh, gracious, no. I'm afraid you just aren't that interesting."

"So they just show up when I'm in trouble?"

"No. Didn't no one ever teach you about angels?"

"Not really. You mean they're here now?"

"As plain as the nose on your face."

"Why? Why are they here?"

"It's time." She grinned and turned walking away.

"Time? Time for what?"

"Time for you to listen to your heart, Jim Benson. Time to listen to your heart."

Jim watched the two of them walk away and was beginning to feel a little uneasy. She had just disappeared across the road when a big red Buick with a white top rolled down the driveway. The car stopped in front of him and Mary got out.

"Hi. I just wanted to say good-bye."

"You're leaving already?"

"Yeah, Dad had his interview in the shipyard and Mom isn't feeling very well, so we decided to get back home."

She could see his expression fading.

"I hope to see you again, Jimmy. Have fun at the dance tonight."

"Okay."

Chapter Ten

"Bye."

"Bye, Jim," Karen yelled from the back seat as Mary got in.

Jim just stood there and waved, with the unquestionable feeling that something was terribly wrong all of a sudden. As the car honked and pulled away, he felt like he was going to throw up.

Jim's mom came out of the house at the sound of the car, just in time to see it leaving the driveway. At the same time, an old black woman sat in a rocking chair singing to the oncoming thunder.

"Amazing Grace, how sweet the sound, that saved a wretch like me..."

"Who was that?"

"That was Mary, but now she's gone," Jim said, looking at her the way a son would, wanting her to make it all better.

"Mary? Karen's friend?"

Jim just nodded.

"Was she the little girl who was all wet with you yesterday?"

"Yeah," he answered, watching the last of the car turn the corner toward the bus stop.

"Is that the Mary you were dreaming about the other night? The same one from the hospital? Your wife? Oh, wait. No, it couldn't be—you hadn't even met her yet."

Jim's eyes turned and stared back at his mother, then to her crucifix, then down the driveway toward the car that he could not see but knew was still there. Pieces began to fall into place and all of his memories merged with one another. In an instant he remembered who he was. There was no confusion. In the dream, Mary was leaving again and Jim understood that he didn't belong here any longer; he never did. He was nothing more than a strange visitor whose time to leave had come. In his heart he knew that he did not want another love, or to wait and watch his true love grow up. He wanted to be with her. Though the road was certain enough, the path to it was not. Perhaps if he trusted, trusted in God again, he might find his way. Trust. He had to trust.

"I once was lost, but now am found, was blind but now I see..."

Mrs. Benson watched the way her son's eyes changed as he looked back at her. They now were the eyes of a man, telling her that everything was going to be all right. They were soft, gentle eyes.

"I love you, Ma." Jim's feet cleared the stone wall as he headed across the field to intercept his life. "MARY! MARY!" he yelled, but the clapping of thunder drowned his voice.

"'Twas grace that taught my heart to fear, and grace my fears relieved..."

Whizzing through the small pine trees toward the clearing, Jim almost flattened the priest, who stood as if he were expecting the boy all along. Spinning around Michael, Jim kept going, now fixating on the car just turning onto Shore Road.

"MARY! W-A-I-T!" he screamed. His voice bounced off of the windows of the old Buick, now rolled up to protect its occupants from the angel tears falling from the sky.

"How precious did that grace appear, the hour I first believed..."

Jim reached the last wall, jumping for the one last chance he had at his Mary, but he was too late. The Buick rumbled past him without a thought. Too late for Mary, too late for Jim, but not too late for the Ford that slammed into the boy's body, hurling him through the air.

"Through many dangers, toils and snares, I have already come..."

Jim's mother reacted to the screeching of tires. Horrified, she knew what had happened and followed her son's invisible trail to find him.

The desperate attempt to avoid the boy had sent the Ford into the stone wall, where the driver lay unconscious over the steering wheel. Jimmy lay sprawled out across the road, face up.

FLASH!

"'Tis grace hath brought me safe thus far and grace will lead me home..."

The blue was back and Jim could see better now and hear with perfect clarity all of the voices that overlapped one another.

"Harrison Memorial, be advised we have a possible donor."

"And one and two and three and four and five and breathe. Nothing. Dial us up to three sixty and hit him again."

"CLEAR!"

"Ma'am...you folks...you're going to have to stand back."

"He's my son, Jimmy. Please let me through."

FLASH!

Jimmy's eyes were blinking in spasms, unable to move because of the pain in his chest. Michael was bent over him, waiting. Light drizzle filled the air and Jimmy started to cough. He could hear his mother screaming his name somewhere in the distance but his eyes were on the calico cat peering at him from underneath the Ford pickup. Everything was coming clear to him now.

"I...I thought," he whispered, "that it was a wish, you know, a wish for things to be different, but I'm wrong aren't I?"

The priest stared back into the boy's eyes.

"I'm not really here, am I? This is something like a distorted reflection of my life, isn't it?" He paused while the rain began to crash down around them, his mother's voice coming closer. "But you're real, aren't you?"

Michael nodded back, still without expression.

Blood trickled from the boy's broken nose. "I'm dead, aren't I? I'm really not here, am I? I'm really in a wreck outside of my shack, and the voices that I hear are from them, right?

"When we've been there ten thousand years, Bright shining as the sun..."

Michael spoke. "Dead? I'm not sure what you speak of. The Son of Man is the God of the living, James. It is not possible to be anything else but changed in His presence."

"He teaches the dead how to live?"

"He teaches the deaf how to hear. Listen and all things will become clear."

"Who are you, Michael?"

"I am the sword of the Christ."

"Help me understand, please."

Michael closed his eyes.

FLASH!

"It's no good. It's been too long. He's gone, for Christ's sake. Let him go."

"Negative. You do your job and let the hospital decide. Harrison Hospital, be advised that we have extraction and will be en route, ETA 12 minutes. Get these people back!"

Jim could see the fireman with the hot breath looking at him. He could see everyone around him as if he were floating above them. His mother was there, old and frail, with arms crossed and tears running down her cheeks. Small groups of his neighbors stood, whispering with one another while lines of traffic waited.

FLASH!

"Jim." It was Michael again.

Gasping for air he tried to focus. "I was wrong, so very wrong. I'm so sorry I said those things to you."

The boy lay there looking up into the man's eyes as the ground around them exploded into water droplets. Michael moved himself over to shield Jimmy's face.

"I just wanted to start over. That's all. Have things be the way that they were—the way that I thought that they should be. I wanted it because I thought that I had ruined my life beyond repair—so bad that it couldn't be fixed. Michael, I was wrong. I didn't look for an answer, but I should have."

"An answer?"

"Jesus…I should have wished to touch Him, to have Him heal me."

"A prayer?"

"Yeah."

"When you wish, Jim, it is a desire to be in control. A prayer is to trust in God. Do you see the difference?"

Jimmy tried to nod with an audible, "Yes."

The priest held out his hands. "Touch these, these hands that have touched the hands, that have touched Jesus. Believe in them and be reborn. Believe them and go home. Your life awaits you."

Jim looked at Michael's hands held out in front of him. "I'm so afraid to go back. I don't know if I can."

"Trust, Jim. Trust."

"But it was me all along. I was the one who left. I walked out on her and broke a promise that burns my soul."

"Forgiveness can quench the fires of hell."

"Will my life be changed…is it a different one that awaits me?"

Chapter Ten

"It is the same. You are the only one who can change it. You will have the same gift that every man has: the gift of a new day, a new beginning."

Jim's eyes grew wide looking at the palms. Blood began to drip from the center of each palm before him, even though there was no apparent injury. He realized that he was no longer seeing Michael's hands. The ones before him were the hands of God himself.

As Jim's hands made contact with them, he started to cry. "Oh, I...I can hear. It's not about me, is it? My life."

"No, Jim." Michael smiled. "It is not. It is about following your heart and living the greatest commandment of all, that of Love. It is sharing what you have of yourself and not being concerned about what you possess or what you feel you do not possess, for there is nothing material on this earth that is yours— not truly. Let not the sum of what you acquire for yourself outweigh that which you give to others. Remember that you are but a visitor in this place whose time to leave will come. Do you understand me?"

"Yes."

"Jim, you once walked away from your life because you were afraid of the opinion of another. You are who you are in your heart, and that will always remain. Your body is merely a vehicle made to follow its desires. Guard those desires well and choose them wisely." With that the priest pulled his hands away from the boy and closed his eyes.

For a brief moment Jim was whole, not just physically, but spiritually. In that instant, he wondered if God spoke to each and every soul on earth differently, so that they would also be able to understand. That is, if they would only listen.

"We've no less days to sing God's praise, than when we first begun."

The attending fireman had taken his eyes off of Jim for only a second, and when he looked back he fell away in utter disbelief. The patient was not only sitting up, but soaking wet as well.

Two Eyes watched from underneath what was left of New Old Blue, her ears going up and down, up and down. When Jim made eye contact with her, she came out and licked the inside of his ear with her famous "I'm-glad-that-you're-not-so-stupid-after-all" lick.

Lying back down on the stretcher, he looked up at her.

"Thank you for being there for me. It was as plain as the nose on my face."

Two Eyes barked and pulled away, running across the field toward an old red Cadillac that seemed to have been waiting all along. As the emergency workers gained enough courage to attend to their patient again, Jim's eyes found his mother and nodded to her. It was his way of saying that everything was going to be all right.

A thin smile crept to her face and the old woman nodded back to her son, reaching for a little gold cross that she had worn so long ago—which now could only be seen in her mind.

Credits

"Into every intelligence there is a door which is never closed, through which the creator passes."
Reprinted by permission of the publishers from
ESSAYS OF RALPH WALDO EMERSON, Second
Series, edited by Alfred R. Ferguson and Jean Ferguson
Carr, Cambridge, Mass.: The Belknap Press of Harvard
University Press, Copyright © 1979, 1983, 1987 by the
President and Fellows of Harvard College.

WEDDING SONG (There Is Love),
© 1971 (Renewed) Public Domain Foundation, Inc.
All Rights Reserved.   Used by Permission.
WARNER BROS. Publications U.S. INC., Miami, FL.
33014

WHAT A WONDERFUL WORLD, by George David
Weiss and Bob Thiele © 1967 Range Road Music Inc.
and Quartet Music Inc. © Renewed 1995 George David

"With only a little sense you will walk on the main
road. The only fear will be straying from it. It is easy to
stay on the main road. But people seem to love being
led astray."
From KUNG FU MEDITATIONS & Chinese
Proverbial Wisdom.
Thor Publishing Company, Ventura CA. Used by
permission.

Some of the terms used in this book came from the
"Glossary" of the "Vietnam Veterans Home Page" at:
http://www.vietvet.org/glossary.htm

Special thanks to the family of Wayne Stanford who
authored GLIMPSES OF MANSON HISTORY.

Acknowledgements

I would like to publicly recognize and express my utmost appreciation to the following friends who have made an invaluable contribution to the creation of this story:

My darling wife and children, who God sent to me, full of patience and understanding.
My mother and father, who instilled in me the belief that I could attain anything.
The American Book Publishing Group, for taking a chance on an unknown writer.
My editor, Leslie Sellers, and my copyeditor, Krista Smith, who have changed a story into a book.
Mr. Doug Wallis, "For here you will find the words of wisdom that you so kindly spoke, and here I will echo them to the world."
Mary Plichta and Anja Wallis, "The Sisters" who truly teach through example.

Joe and Esther Riggs, for their continual love and support.
Carol Ann Campbell, "The Angel With the Pale Green Eyes."
Teri Fink, for teaching me how to chisel.
Bobbie Kenagy, "Mum," "The Traveling Saint."
Cora Hartley, "The Music of Manson."
Robert Shinkoskey, for his heartfelt encouragement.
The talented Chris Raines at SUNGRAPHIC DESIGN LABS, and his lovely wife Shar.
Dick and Phyllis Charles, who have cheered every step of the way.

And, of course, Gail Rice, for being my friend, even after thirty years.

An extra special thanks to the individuals who granted copyright permission for the use of their words. I know how hard you work, and I appreciate your kindness.

About the Author

Vic Peters makes his home in Manson, Washington, and is married with two children. The son of a Naval officer, he spent his childhood in various locations throughout the United States, including Cape Neddick, Maine, the setting for a portion of this story. Vic is a full-time cabinetmaker, who, in addition to writing, also enjoys hunting and fishing.

Learn more about the author and the unique aspects of this story at www.marysfield.com.